BACK
TO THE
HOOD

A GANGSTER'S VISION

by
RICARDO PIMENTEL

Edited by
AMY CECILIA

CONTENTS

After 11 years locked up, Franchize was ready to do right by his family. However, the streets kept calling his name and forcing his hand. Torn between doing the right thing and protecting himself above all, Franchize realizes that this is how it will always be when you're back in the hood.

CHAPTER 1

Franchize walked down Steinway Street. He couldn't help noticing how vivid the colors were today. The sun's gleam off the windows he passed by gave off brilliant shades of gold and orange. A soft breeze with the scent of spring kissed his skin. People walked by without the faintest idea in the world about who he was nor did they care for that matter. This was New York City. The smells, the people, the places. Enough activities to consume a man's curiosity for years nonstop. The sights, food and clothes always stood out.

He started to wonder why he was walking down the block. He tried to remember what street he was on but couldn't. The entire time saying to himself that this street was familiar. Franchize felt a weird sense of shame because he didn't remember. He tried to sort out the smells but before he could put a name to them, they slipped through the cracks in his mind. The colors started to shift with more frequency. The entire color spectrum ricocheted off of anything with a surface. Franchize couldn't help thinking he was going blind as panic started to set in.

"Count, on the count! Lights on, standing!" Reality felt like a bucket of cold water thrown on Franklin Montenegro's face. This has been the torture he has lived with for the past 11 years. Prison. "Why?" he asked himself, "Why am I still here when my lesson has been learned?"

Franchize focused on getting himself together after being reminded yet again of his prison ID number. He went through his daily mantra. *"My past is the past. I am the greatest force paving the way for my future"*. Repeating the cornerstone of his rehabilitation, the tension started to ease its way out of him. The pent up stress began to ebb as relaxation found its way into his limbs. Feeling the sharpness of a clear mind kicked off the day's routine. The temptation or laziness crept into his head then he shook it out. He understood that in the wolf's den, being on point was the bare minimum needed to navigate the traps and snake pits littered throughout prison life like potholes on NYC streets.

He put his Hot Pot to boil the water he needed for his coffee. While brushing his teeth, Franchize organized the day's tasks. Trying to control as much of his life as possible after becoming state property was of paramount importance to him. With all the time he had on his hands, Franchize made sure he studied on the details. He needed to be shrewd and cautious at the same time. Over the years, he became able to navigate the organized chaos that is the New York State Department of Corrections and Community Supervision. Before leaving his cell, there were two things that had to be done- become one with his caffeine and work out.

Breakfast was uneventful. Most people were half asleep except for the dangerous ones. The Correctional Officers were just plain harassing anyone they felt gave them the smallest of reasons. The mess hall was a huge room full of tables that held rows of stools bolted to the floor where you sat in the order you came in. Once you got to the serving section, you picked up a tray and were served your slop. Today was Monday which meant the nastiest oatmeal you ever tasted, 4 slices of bread, and milk. Just like every other Monday.

"Ayo Franchize, slow down!" He looked back and Joey Serrano AKA Blaze was skipping people in line to catch up. "Blaze, one day these pigs are going to pull you over for running all them stop signs and red lights to give you more than a ticket". Blaze just laughed.

"Franchize, you already know I don't give a fuck about anything. These crackers pull me over and act up, they gonna get some act right outta me. Plus I ain't seen Robo Cop. Did you spot Officer Delany today?" Blaze looked around for us prisoner's biggest headache.

"You slippin' Blaze. You weren't even sure he was working before you jumped out the window. Nah, I ain't seen him".

"Good, I got something lined up for us in the yard."

"No, you don't. Us equals me and you and I told ya I am falling back from everything that can get me trapped off. I got my release date coming up in a couple of months. If I fuck up, I lose that. Forget it Blaze. It ain't worth it. I want a beer and a steak. It's quiet, ya dig?"

"Big bro, this is what we do. We turn it up. Have lames burning it up. This Recreation aide job we got has us in the yard for a reason. I know you ain't acting brand new. Let's paper chase".

Franchize gave Blaze an ice grill that spoke all the words necessary. Seeing that he wasn't getting anywhere with his boy, he spun off after breakfast. "*If Franchize wanted to play Mr. Righteous now, so be it*", thought Blaze. "*Who can stop me from doing what I do alone anyways? All I been doing is splitting profits with Franchize over the years. It was time for a come up*".

It was already engraved in Blaze's mind that he was going to take the hit on Fats before he consulted Franchize. 14 grams of weed and 10 packs of Newports would ensure he would be blazing every day for at least a week. All that needed to be done was a cut to Fats face to make sure the administration moved him out of the jail. Now that Franchize fell back, the whole ounce as payment sounded great.

Fats owned Big Boy $500 which is bad for business. It's a sign of weakness if Big Boy doesn't move on him. Blaze loved the routine. Someone always took more product than they could afford. Big Boy paid 28 grams of good green to clean up debts when someone defaulted. The rest of the people that owned would see what happened when they played games and the cycle would repeat itself. Blaze didn't understand why Big Boy continued to let people get so deep into debt. It didn't matter because he got to cash in.

After the equipment was handed out, Franchize headed towards the weight pit. He did calisthenics in the morning and weights in the afternoon. The new routine started when he realized he was less than 90 days to go home. Today his focus was off. His attention on Blaze allowed him to study the way he interacted with everyone. Franchize pretty much got the gist of what was going down. He also noticed when Big Boy passed Blaze the package. With the people involved and the way Blaze was acting, tit couldn't be anything less than a hit. Watching Blaze go to the stash spot only solidified his suspicions.

Franchize felt all types of conflicting emotions. He did not want to let his comrade go on a dangerous mission by himself, but he could no longer deny himself the freedom his very essence craved. After his inner battle played out, he chose not to act. Priorities were organized already. Franchize was a realist and hard on the people he cared for when it became appropriate. Understanding these events are a fork in the road with different paths being chosen didn't make it any easier. He felt bad about his choice, but why was that uneasy feeling creeping into the back of this mind telling him something wasn't right?

Blaze around as if he became larger than life with every step. A magnet for attention. He loved for people to call his name and to be recognized as a shooter. People like to have Blaze around. He didn't care for rules and laughed when awkward situations came up, always easing the tension. His aura and well practiced demeanor was designed to put people at ease. Everyone was comfortable around Blaze. They also knew if you crossed him, he would cut or stab you. That mixture of charisma and danger sparked a curiosity encouraging you into finding out more about him. But when you did find out about Blaze's life, it made you wonder how he held a smile on his face.

Blaze grew up poor. Foster homes. Group homes. Juvenile Detention Centers. Adolescent prison time. Then at 18, a robbery went badly and he shot the owners of his girlfriend's building on rent collection day. What made matters worse was that he hit a blank when it was supposed to be a jackpot. He knew nothing of checks and money orders. He looked at it as monopoly money. The petty cash the Guzmans carried only infuriated Blaze even more. The man moved on step towards him breaking the order not to move and Blaze let fly eight bullets from his High Point 9 mm hand gun. Five hit the husband. As he fell, 3 hit his wife that was right behind him. All in broad daylight. The man died and the woman barely survived. Since the District Attorney's office offered him 25 years to life as a plea bargain, Blaze took it to trial. When the guilty verdict came down with a sentencing of 40 years to life. Blaze accepted his fate. It really didn't bother him that much. He had nobody in the courtroom for him anyway. He never knew his parents and at this stage in his life he didn't want to know them. Being through the difficult situations alone made him the way he was.

Blaze felt free of any and all responsibilities after sentencing. No more having to worry about bills. No rent, electricity, phones or even having to worry about where his next meal was going to come from. Three hots and a cot until the sun burns out. He hustled up a radio and a T.V. Over the years, he tweaked his cell until it felt like his own mini penthouse. Blaze didn't want to change. He knew what he was feeling. To express it to the world would make him look insane. On the street, he had nothing and was a nobody. In prison all he had was his name He knew how to make his name ring bells behind these prison walls. Therefore, becoming a legend in the system became a top priority. His name would shine through committing prison crime.

CHAPTER 2

"Yo Scrappy, what's goody bro?" Fats asked his little homeboy. He thought his little man looked distraught, possibly nervous for some reason. At 5 foot 3 inches tall weighing 125 lbs soaking wet, Fats knew almost anything could scare Scrappy. Nobody ever noticed him all that much. He was always quiet and Fats wouldn't have even known of Scrappy's existence if he didn't remind him that he used to date Scrappy's older sister Evelyn. Fats put up with having Scrappy's dark skinned chickenpox-marked face around. It became only natural for Fats to have ulterior motive by keeping Scrappy close. He wanted to get at his sister Eve again. This way she could come see him on visits and take care of him. Food packages and money in his account went a long way in Prison. By what he got off of Scrappy every month suggested she did a lot for him. Fats wanted in, but when Scrappy put him on the phone with Eve, she blatantly disrespected him. She jumped out the window talking out the side of her neck like that. Nobody talked to him in that manner and got away with it. He felt like he made her who she was. Evelyn hit a lot of nerves when she was shooting off her cock holster. He didn't like hearing the truth about himself so he kept repeating to himself that she was nobody until her accusations regarding what he did to her were non-existent.

Now plan B for Scrappy became on deck. There were a couple of homothugs willing to pay for a shot at little Scrappy. They wouldn't dare go at someone down with a team. They also knew though that Fats was past due on a big debt to Big Boy. The offer of $300 to set his little man up couldn't be passed up in Fats' eyes. They knew he was greedy and as morally bankrupt as they came. So the deal was set in stone. In exchange for $300 worth of heroine, Fats has to send Scrappy to the back of the recreation shack. All Scrappy needed to know was that he was meeting with someone that had something important for him. Scrappy looked up to Fats and would do almost anything for him. He knew Fats was his protection in this jungle. Keeping his eyes and ears open was all he had to offer Fats. So when he came across suspicious activity, the first thing he always did was pull Fats' coat.

"Big homie, I gots to holla at you in private. Serious."

"Aight lil' man."

When Scrappy had Fats by himself, he told him how he saw Big Boy give Blaze something and how he heard Big Boy say Fats' name. Fats wasn't slow in connecting the dots. He never had any intentions of paying Big Boy, but he didn't expect Big Boy to be crazy enough to go after him. Fats was more fat than muscle, but his size gave him a strength to be respected. Blaze was a lightweight, his same exact height. With this new information, Fats would take advantage of the situation.

CHAPTER 3

Blaze's light skinned complexion warmed under the sun. Spring was in full bloom. He looked left then right. Scanning the less populated spots in the yard, he remembered that the best advantage was always the element of surprise. He knew that when your victim doesn't see it coming, they froze. Every time. Usually, Franchize rode safety. He had a knack for delivering one hitter quitters for the select few who would come at their assailant instead of retreating for medical attention. Blaze wasn't concerned with Fats. He looked like a bird and the only real nigga he fucked with to come out of Queens was Franchize. His boy was the exception to the Brooklyn Knight circle.

Knowing speed was on his side, he put his red sweater on to camouflage any possible blood stains.

Red is a popular color and it would help him blend into the masses of people wearing it. The goal was to clap Fats, change, and then go back to his work station. The long sleeved green shirt he wore underneath would be warm enough until he got back to his cell.

While approaching Fats, something felt wrong. He had a certain look on him that read as if he was on guard. After being in prison a couple of years, you became a master of reading body language. Now he would have to look for the edge, the chink in Fats' armor. Not a simple hit and run anymore. Then Fats' gave him the best opening possible. If the shoe was on the other foot, Fats for sure would have gotten hip to what he was planning on doing. It became a walk in the park.

Fats pointed in the direction they would walk to roll up and smoke. Blaze got hype and said he had a little bit of bud to add to make the blunt fatter. He couldn't help smiling and talking. Little did he know that one of the oldest tricks in the book would be used against him. Fats passed Blaze the cigar and a little sack of bud inside of toilet tissue. The time it took Blaze to realize that there was no bud in the toilet tissue cost him dearly. He didn't see that they had just crossed into the blind spot behind the outdoor showers. All of a sudden, it felt like a cuffed slap came across his face. When he looked up, he saw Fats dropping the top of a can through the grate beneath where he was standing. Little Scrappy crept up from behind and pushed Blaze straight into a right hook from Fats. Dazed on the floor, Blaze couldn't help scolding himself. He froze and now a bird could say he shot him. He tried to get up but it was useless. He was dizzy and it had him all over the place.

It happened quickly and in between one of Franchize's sets. Noticing what was going down, he moved in their direction without thinking. Natural reflexes worked for this type of situation. The distance he was trying to cover seemed further than usual. His mind worked overtime while the world around him slowed down. Before he got there, Fats got away and Blaze was being picked up by the C.O.'s. He was handcuffed and on his way out to the infirmary.

Rage boiled beneath Franchize's skin. Heated couldn't describe the flames that clouded his eyes. He saw blood dripping from everyone involved in what happened to his boy. Subconsciously, his reasoning kicked started a breathing pattern to help calm him. His mind pushed his daily mantra through his darker thoughts. *"My past is the past. I am the greatest force paving the way for my future."*

He started walking the yard. Focusing on memories of the fun times Blaze and he enjoyed over the last two years in this prison brought to surface emotions that were buried. He pushed those emotions back down. This is no place to let a weakness like that show. He could feel eyes on him wondering what he was going to do. This is where they met and his gut feeling was saying this was where they part. Clenching his jaw, he asked himself why he felt this was a coward's way out. Loyalty, and respect for his comrade in the struggle surfaced. He couldn't let his boy go out like that. However, responsibility is a two-edged sword. His desire and need to walk upon streets were strong. Images of his family expecting him home soon rocked him in another direction. The see-saw effect was making him sick.

Franchize was torn between two worlds. One way or another he was going to have to figure out this madness. He understood that there is no half-stepping. It's all or nothing. His mind started to clear. The ingrained patience prison installed in him gave him an idea. The best thing to do right now was to feel the vibe of certain people and check out the atmosphere of the prison. Time would answer his question and direct the path of his next move.

CHAPTER 4

The next day Franchize went through his routine. He felt something was wrong at breakfast. Too many quick glances in his direction. He knew people were going to be acting funny style because his boy got twisted in the yard and everybody was waiting to see what he was going to do. Franchize didn't even answer the people who were calling to him on the gat last night. He needed time to reflect.

Knowing human nature made these men nosey in an environment meant for people to mind their business let him see things in a new light. They were digging for information to use as gossip or against him. Over the last couple of years, he accumulated the right amount of enemies and haters to make the hardest of criminals wince, but it is what it is.

Blaze had become the politician by proxy. He had all the friends. Franchize's anti-social demeanor made it easy for Blaze to dump the blame and problems for situations on his lap. Friends with people did not add up in Franchize's life. In this melting pot of criminals, you couldn't tell who was who. It was better in his world to stick with one person he could *almost* trust. Now that Blaze was gone, he had to deal with the jailhouse politics. He almost missed Big Boy's approach. It was only a matter of time before a man like this would weasel his way in to use this situation as leverage in his favor.

"Yo Franchize, what's shaking?" Big Boy asked as he looked around.

"Ain't shit Big Boy; what's up?"

"Straight to business; I like that. Check it- your boy Blazed fucked up and a deal is a deal. You picking up what I'm putting down?"

"Yeah, you got your hands full with Fats now," Franchize said with a smug smile on his face.

"No, not really. You do." Big Boy changed his stance as his team started to flank him. The yard started to quiet down as all eyes stared at the conflict emerging by the recreation shack. Franchize instantly understood there was no winning on his behalf from what was unfolding.

"Why would Fats be my problem? You dealt with Blaze. Blaze is gone. It looks to me that Fats is your problem."

"That's where you're wrong Franchize. Blaze said you and him were going to handle the contract. I even gave him enough greenery to cover both of you. So you have been paid for a contract. Your word is all you have and your man gave it." Big Boy stared at Franchize waiting for a reaction.

The seriousness of Big Boy's words started to sink in as the situation became clear. "Hey Big Boy, we never talked about this personally. Whatever you and Blaze did was between you and him. He ain't coming back and I know where his stash is at so I can give you that back and we're all set."

"I don't think you understand Franchize. Ya mans word is your word. Am I my brother's keeper and all that good shit. I don't want the work back. My contract is to be fulfilled. If not, we coming for you first. Ya dig what I'm saying?"

"Big Boy, let me get back to you in a couple of days so I can let you know how I feel about this new development."

"Nah, you got 48 hours to handle what you gots to handle" With that Big Boy and his team started moving away and the dangerous tension in the air between the two most dangerous men in the prison started to recede.

Everyone knew Big Boy was a lifer. He had no possibility of parole. Having a cop body was a sure way of guaranteeing you would never go home. He knew that. That's why he was so violent. He only changed his approach to committing the violence himself when he monopolized this prison's drug game. Clinton Correctional Facility has over 2,000 convict behind its walls. A rich environment of drug addicts and corruption. The dealers Big Boy has working for him don't want to entertain the idea of fucking up. They know he wouldn't think twice about killing a man in prison.

Big Boy started using his reputation and position. By thinking things through, he put a portion of his profits to dictate violence. The more bloodshed he accomplished, the more excited he became. This was all a game to him. His current form of entertainment. Given the prison's high minority population, he blended in and out of crowds like a chameleon in a forest. He had unremarkable features- not quite dark skinned, not quite brown skinned, average height and weight. His eyes held that hard edge like a chipped stone. It gave you the impression that you should back off. Big Boy's body was only a shell that contained evil. Watching people struggle with immense pain was the only thing that gave him joy.

"Ayo Moe, Peaches, you got Fats' lil' man lined up?"

"Yeah Big Boy. We all set to go," Moe answered before he spun off with Peaches.

Setting up entertainment with Fats' lil' man was easy. Making sure Fats didn't get paid that $300 was even easier. All Big Boy had to do was be careful with jailhouse politics. He didn't want too many people to know how extreme his tastes were when it came to watching the pain in a man's face. Just watching the violation would arouse him, but that was it. He didn't need or want anything more from the situation besides visual stimulation. The rush was what he needed.

CHAPTER 5

ranchize paced his cell. His thought fought each other. He could destroy his name by pulling a stunt, but he knew he couldn't live with himself for going the coward's way out. Going to the police was out of the question. He hated that no matter how much he tried to retire from the game, it pulled him back in from all directions. He has a responsibility to his family. They hurt everyday knowing he was behind these walls, yet Franchize prayed they understood if worse came to worst. The only option he saw was gripping up with his chin up. Fats was by all accounts an easier target than Big Boy. Going after Fats would allow him to get revenge for his boy and get Big Boy off of his back. As Franchize mind worked out all the ways to take care of Fats, one stood out above all.

Some men were creatures of habit and this time it would hurt Fats.

Franchize woke up in his element. He was fully focused. Once he got into the yard, he moved with purpose. Going to the stash spot, he fished out an ice pick and the greenery Big Boy paid to Blaze. He quit smoking over six months ago and didn't have a need for anything. Spotting Chico crossing the yard on the flats, he approached him.

"Hey Chico, what's up with you?"

"Nothing much. Blaze sends his love. I'm still a porter on D block and ya boy is driving me crazy."

"Yeah, that's Blaze. If I got a kite for him, can you make it happen?"

"All day. I clean the company. Why; what's up?"

"Take this and tell Blaze I said to take care of you for your troubles."

"No doubt big bro. I'm gonna make sure this is a touchdown. This is an official real nigga move."

"You already know. I gots to bust a move. Be easy bro." Franchize moved away and watched Chico go up to his court.

"Yo Fats, I got the bat," Scrappy said. The softball game was set to start soon. "Scrap, you always getting the shitty bat. I told you to get the red one." Before Scrappy could respond, Fats moved quickly towards the recreation shack to get the red bat. "Scrap go behind the rec shack and pick up what Moe got for me right now. Quit wasting time lil' nigga."

Franchize saw Fats getting closer to the recreation shack window as the line moved. "Guata, hold me down. You already know what it is."

Guatemala was paramilitary in his home country. He was a real killer and didn't like too many people. He didn't talk much so flying under the radar was easy for him. He looked like a regular dude from south of the border until you crossed him. That's when he went berserk in the blink of an eye. He knew how to move so he kept lookout for the C.O.'s and continued to hand out the equipment to keep the flow going. Franchize slid out the side door. Being tall and wide shouldered made it hard for him to sneak up on someone. Speed would keep the element of surprise on his side. Sharp reflexes and flash decisions needed to be made.

Franchize looked around the side of the shack and saw Fats pulling up to the window. Predator mode kicked in. Fast as lightening, Franchize came around the corner as Fats had his hand extended to retrieve the red bat after exchanging the one he had. Before Fats could move his head towards the movement he saw out of the corner of his eye, he was stabbed twice. Franchize felt the ice pick puncture Fats' lung on his right side. He kept moving right past Fats. Guata turned the bat around to place a powerful jab to Fats' temple since there was no room to get a swing in. Fats stumbled backwards until he fell on his ass.

Adrenaline pumping, Franchize turned the other side of the shack wall and headed towards the back so he could stash the pick and enter trough the rear. What he found raised the hairs on his arms and neck. He couldn't believe the sick shit his eyes were witnessing.

Big Boy was off to the side sitting on a crate and two known booty bandits had a young brother bent over a workout bench. He was bleeding and crying from a face that showed fear. Franchize paused for a second to take the scene in. one man had his knee on Scrappy's back and pulled on his hair so his head tilted up to look at Big Boy. The other man stood behind Scrappy with his pants around his ankles, meat in hand with his other hand on little Scrappy's lower back ready to change the young brother's life completely until he noticed Franchize standing there.

"Peaches, let him up," Franchize growled.

Peaches moved with quickness off of Scrappy. He was scared of ice picks and on top of that, he lived on the same company as Franchize.

Moe on the other hand was furious. He flipped little Scrappy over and grabbed him by the neck, twisting the smaller man until he came face to face with Moe's meat. Scrappy's hands shot up and closed around Moe's wrists trying to break free. Franchize moved. All the anger he had within fueled his speed. Moe tried to shift his footing and fell on his ass as Franchize snuffed him with a left. Scrappy fell on top of Moe. Franchize started circling looking for a clean shot with the pick.

Big Boy got up and said, "Enough! Peaches get lost. Moe fall back. Franchize, this never happened, right?" Heart racing, adrenaline pumping, Franchize wanted to say fuck everything and kill all three of these bozos right now. Instead of acting on impulse, he calmed himself down, made eye contact with Big Boy and said, "I was never here".

Big Boy smiled and said, "Good". Then he walked away like nothing ever happened. Franchize spun off to put the pick away. Coming out the shack where his stash was, he saw little Scrappy surrounded by correctional officers. They looked around for a weapon and instead of finding it, they found an abused young man. Franchize could hear the young man telling the C.O.'s that he wanted Protective Custody. He was giving up names and a description of what happened to him! He couldn't hear the rest as he melted back into the shack. Franchize shook his head and said to himself that this madness was almost over.

Shortly after that Blaze got word back to Franchize expressing gratitude and letting him know real niggas do real things. The messages didn't stop coming and he knew it was Blaze being who he was, loving to shoot shit from his lips. Franchize just smiled.

Playing politician with the Q-Boro peoples became a necessity because of the Fats hit. Being both from Queens made the situation and conflict die down after a few days. But in the back of his mind, he knew that eventually he would bump into Fats at parole. What's done is done and when the time comes to cross that road, he would like a posted court.

The rest of the days left Franchize tried to get his thoughts organized. It turned into a time of preparation. Before he knew it, it was the night before his release. Franchize couldn't sleep. His mind raced. He kept thinking about all of the possibilities. The what if, could be, and maybe's with everything in between. Eleven and a half years straight without the luxuries life had to offer were frustrating. Just as he started to drift off, "Montenegro, get up. Go up front; you're out of here. You don't leave a mess in that cell either, you hear?" Franchize smiled saying, "Yeah, I am ready to go right now. All set officer."

CHAPTER 6

After being processed out, he stepped on the concrete for the first time in a long time a as free man. The sun shined down on him and a warm breeze lifted his spirits. The feeling was even better than he ever imagined. Franchize wanted to take the trip home by himself. He needed to truly recognize the gift of freedom that was bestowed on him. To pay attention to the sights and the flow of life. Of actually being on his own and getting things done. For the first couple of hours of freedom, he needed to be by himself.

His bus pulled into New York City that evening. He heard the person across from him playing "Empire State of Mind" by Alicia Keys and Jay-Z. Goosebumps rose on his arm and that's when he finally felt it. That moment he waited for without even knowing. The realization that he was home. This is his backyard and everyone else was visiting. It became time to get money the right way. A new spin on a spinning platform formed in his mind and now it felt almost at hand.

On his train ride home, he couldn't help but notice the ladies getting n and off the train. To the trained eye, you couldn't miss the fact that Franchize had state clothes on and his glow screamed "just released from prison!" This thick, exotic beauty happened to step on the train and he couldn't help but plot on this eye candy. Franchize didn't want to indulge so soon after release but this would be a challenge to see if he still had it. She stood in front of him so he got up and said, "Excuse me sweetheart, would you like a seat?"

Misha grew up in the hood and knew a jail bird when she saw one. Too muscular to have only done a year and his clothes spoke of his recent release from state prison. A cute man, but she had too much going on for her right now for a sorry distraction. No matter how sexy. These jail birds only thought about themselves and were emotional wrecks. Way too volatile for her tastes. Temptation had her considering a one night stand, but that thought ended when the image of a stalker popped up. She recently opened her salon and worked 12 hour days. Her business became her everything and if she wanted to continue to be successful, she had to stay on track. She chose to ignore Mr. Temptation.

He came up with something that was persistent, yet not too overbearing. "¿Bella, hablas español?" he asked. "No? Você fala Português? No? parlez-vous Français? Is that a smile? Español, Português, or Français?

On a whim, Franchize showed her the sign for hello and she looked at him like he was crazy Misha knew for sure now he was a dud. Trying to impress her with a gang banging sign is a no-no. She should've known it. Misha stepped to the side a little on the crowded train to further show her disinterest. When she looked back to make sure he didn't follow her, a little old white lady was throwing up signs with who she thought was gang banging. Now that Misha was paying attention, she could tell that his signing was limited to a couple of words, but the older woman smiled anyways and they both laughed. The woman's laugh was quiet and warming. His was a majestic and genuine sound that made her feel as if she was missing out on something, but that thought broke up when the train pulled up to her stop. She started to go down the stairs, but something told her to look back. When she did, she almost fell because Mr. Temptation was right behind her! Thank God he grabbed her by the waist to steady her. Misha was surprised by the strength of his arm at first and then of how gentle his touch became as it lingered a moment. It made her reconsider her previous judgments. Breathlessly she said "Thank you" and kept it moving before the desire of more contact with Mr. Temptation devoured her.

Franchize smiled and went his own way. He decided to walk home since it wasn't that far. He traversed the familiar blocks and a feeling of nostalgia flooded his senses. As he got closer to his block, he saw a familiar face. Standing in front of the bodega was Flaco. A slim Spanish brother the same age as Franchize, 31, but looking a good 10 years older. Franchize paid closer attention and noticed the younger brothers in all of their flash gear in the cut laughing at Flaco. Damn, it was one of the good homies from back in the day asking for a dollar. It hurt Franchize to watch the scene unfolding in front of his eyes. Knowing Flaco used to be able to flip thousands of dollars in crack every night no matter if it was raining or snowing and in the end, became reduced to begging for a dollar set a fire in Franchize's gut. Everything changed out here and he had to remind himself that all of these blocks no longer belonged to him.

Flaco without looking into Franchize's face asked him for a dollar. When a hundred dollar bill popped up in his hand, he looked into the man's face and went pale. He couldn't help stuttering, "M-m-my G-god!". Taking a moment to calm himself he asked, "Franchize, is that you big homie?" Franchize nodded and looked him in the eye. "Flaco, what's good brother? Give your boy a hug!"

The youngsters off to the side started to laugh. A really bold one came forward saying, "Ah look, a crackhead reunion. Flaco you got the rest of that money now so stop wasting my time".

Flaco looked at Chino with despair and said, "Chino, you don't know who this is? Have some respect for one of the hood's original gangsters! This is Franchize Da Don. The one and only. All these blocks…" Franchize interrupted Flaco and said, "It's all good bro. No harm done. I'm easy now anyway".

Chino looked Franchize up and down sizing him up. All that muscle meant nothing. A couple of hot ones would have him dancing. "This is my clock," Chino said.

"It's a nice block in a good spot," Franchize replied.

Chino wanting to further test the waters asked, "You jumping back in the game?" If Franchize tried to take over, Chino knew he had to lay him down instead of losing his cash cow.

"Nah baby bro. I'm done".

Chino, eased by Franchize's reply, gave him a head nod and said, "My big brother Pappo talks about you from time to time. I'll let him know you're home".

Franchize gave everyone a pound and kept it moving. He instantly understood that once he got himself organized, he was moving out the hood. Somebody might try to take a shot at him for some street fame.

His brother and sister arranged a little get together. Alexis lived on the first floor of their mother's brownstone building. The music got him hype. The first person he saw when he walked through the door was Stacey's scandalous ass. The desire to party disappeared with his smile. His number one headache stared back at him. Miss drama queen herself. Stacey didn't get the hint that it was over. She played with his head for too long while he was locked up. One thing Franchize didn't have time for was this girl's games and attention seeking ways. It was time to roast a fat bitch.

"Franchize, you're looking edible," Stacey said.

"Damn, is that really you? What happened? You're looking larger than life, literally."

"Papi, let's go someplace private," Stacey moaned.

"Na, I'm scared you might give me high cholesterol and diabetes," Franchize spun off and started mingling with familiar faces. Stacey's eyes became icy at the public humiliation. If Franchize was going to act like a jerk, she was going to make sure she got back at him.

Alexis pulled Franchize to the side and hugged him. "I got you some clothes. Here are the keys to your apartment. Do you need any money?"

"Nah, I still got some of what they released me with and the fellas been looking out. You seen G Money?"

"Yeah, he is upstairs in your apartment. You know he hates crowds. I want you to meet Pistol. He's the father of my future baby."

"Big bro, 2.24. I salute you," Pistol said.

"You G.M.B?" Franchize asked.

"Yeah yeah, I got one of the general positions under your vision."

"No disrespect, but if you're going to be a father to the seed my sister is carrying, you need to fall back and evolve in another direction."

"It's a Get Money world. But if my Don has a greater vision for me, I must see it as an opportunity. When you get a chance, I gots to bring you up to speed. Nothing is what it used to be."

Franchize went upstairs and walked in on G Money counting money on his table. "My brother, what's shaking? You're looking good," Franchize said.

"We're looking even better now that you're home. This is 20 thousand, a get on your feet gift from the GMB family. Get situated and holla at me. My number is already in your phone," G Money said.

"Yo G Money, good looking on the money, but I want to establish from the gate that I'm inactive and I don't want anything to do with the daily operations. Freedom, parole and a bunch of other responsibilities are going to have my hands tied."

"Don't worry Franchize, when the time is right, you will be ready to rule. Even if it isn't now". G Money came over and gave Franchize a hug then left him alone in his apartment. A feeling that was familiar, yet not so much anymore.

After a bath, Franchize checked the crib and found some old jewelry and a smart phone. Clothes folded neatly and a refrigerator full of food. Taking out a beer and laying back on his bed, he fell asleep with the T.V. on.

He woke up early and worked out so his mind could get today's schedule in order. His priorities were first- parole, then shopping, and a haircut. After he got cleaned up, he had to go holla at a couple of people. Everything was going smoothly until he went to the barbershop. The parole officer wasn't really sweating him too tough. He copped some official gear to go with what the fam put together for him, but his old barber Shawn turned into a bozo. Shawn, known for talking crazy loud when you were right next to him and always exaggerating his movements, started acting weirder. The nervousness began when Gato walked in. Too many questions about what he planned to do. Sloppy work on Shawn and Gato's part. Franchize knew he was out of practice, but some things you never lose. Being on point is one of them. His senses told him these dudes were plotting on him.

Gato is a known rat. Franchize walked the yard with a couple of dudes who had the paperwork on Edwin Sanchez aka Gato. The sad part is that the hood knows he is out here getting money and putting brothers away. They figured if he didn't tell on them yet, he won't. That's where they are wrong. A rat like that waits until the time is right to catch you slipping. He has the N.Y.P.D take out his competition. "Yo Franchize, that's you? Yeah man, you looking food and your cut came out crazy. I wanted to congratulate you for making it home and give you a welcome back present," Gato said while he gave Franchize a pound with about two stacks in it.

On point, Franchize wasn't about to let this lame stroke his ego until he made a mistake. "Good looking bro. This should keep me good 'til my paychecks start coming in. No disrespect, but I gots to run. You be good and I know if I ever need anything I can count on you." No point in turning down free money, but something didn't feel right. Old habits die hard, so Franchize stepped in the check cashing spot and turned the cash into a money order. He felt a lot better after that. It was time to get low, observe, and start working.

CHAPTER 7

Franchize's older brother Negro worked construction and did great for himself. He had never been arrested and his loyalty to his company got him a foreman position years ago. A $22 an hour job waited for Franchize with no questions asked. His big brother wanted the best for him. "Negro, why I didn't see you last night at the get together?" Franchize asked.

"Hey, some of us work, have a wife, and not to forget, kids. Plus, after mom passed away, it's hard for me to stop by the brownstone."

"I hope the fam is good. Thanks for the job. Also, before I forget, do you still have the key?"

"Yeah, Franchize. I kept up the gym membership and did everything you asked. You want the key now?"

"No, big bro. It's better if you hold it. Before I leave, when do I start?"

"6 am. Don't be late your first day at work. Here is my gift to you." Franchize examined the alarm clock his brother passed him and just laughed.

~ ~ ~

The physical work called to Franchize's body. The plumbing work felt honest and kept him busy. The days turned into weeks. His bond with Negro strengthened. He became able to bag mad shorties. Everything was going as planned. A couple of years stacking paper would let him purchase his own condo and open up a business. By then he would be off parole. Life felt great.

~ ~ ~

Stacey picked up the phone and answer the call. "Ayo shorty, what's popping? I got your kite. I'm feeling those pictures too. That was a good look. But the thing is, I don't remember you," Fats said. "I live two blocks from Franchize and I used to hang out with Evelyn. I always had my eye on you and I felt it was time I reach out to you". Stacey hoped the mention of Franchize's name would get him going.

News of the beef reached the streets and she would use it to her advantage.

"Oh really? Damn shorty. You sure know how to make a nigga feel good. I'm short to going home and I'm feeling your swag. I say we build on us and see where this leads…" The wheels in Fats' head started to turn looking for a way to take advantage of the situation.

CHAPTER 8

Franchize had the day off and he shopped with his sister Alexis. Her great fashion sense and enough guts to tell him his choices were too deeply rooted in the past allowed him to compromise on a couple of outfits. It even got to the point where she made him promise to get a manicure every week. Her logic said that after a long week of using and abusing his money getters, it was only right to give them a treat. Plus the ladies would be grateful. Franchize thought it ironic that he hadn't gotten a manicure since his hands were money getters in a different way. Smiling at how he had changed, he walked through the doors of Creations, not knowing his life might change again.

The spot had ladies all over the place, all colors and sizes. With no other straight man in sight, he started feeling himself. Then he saw her- the fly thick exotic beauty from the train. How could he forget? She stood behind the counter talking to another cutie. The nice place seemed new. What surprised Franchize the most was when his sister walked up to the exotic beauty and said, "Misha, what's up sexy?" Everything happened in slow motion after that. He watched Misha do a double take and bring up a smile that reached her eyes. Then the confusion set in when she gazed upon him. The look felt like it lasted forever, but it truly was only a moment in everyone else's life.

"Nothing much but a bunch of work Alexis. I see you're up to a lot," Misha said pointing to Franchize. "Misha, I would like you to meet my brother Franchize. Franchize, this is Misha and Evelyn." Alexis beamed with pride knowing her friends were lusting after her brother. Misha looked Franchize up and down and couldn't place the familiar face. "I must not have seen you in a long time, but I remember you somehow." "Nice to finally meet you, Misha. As for it being a long time, I must ask you if you habla español?"

Misha looked like she just popped a sour patch candy in her mouth. That train scene several of weeks ago became vivid as she looked away in embarrassment. Mr. Temptation had a name and he looked 10 times better. Simple clothes yet everything fit just right making him look sexy and casual at the same time. She didn't like it when men wore tight jeans and the relaxed fit he had on… She was pulled out of her daze when Alexis touched her arm asking, "Is it okay?"

Misha blushed hard and Franchize noticed. "You have to excuse me. I've been out of it all day." Alexis gave Misha a rundown of what they wanted. She agreed to give them the V.I.P treatment. Evelyn reached out her hand for a shake and exclaimed, "Oh my, those are working man hands. I can't help but admire that." Franchize noticed the tightness in Misha's face. He knew right then she was in the bag. All he got done was a manicure and his sister still had a lot to get done. It became a need to get out of dodge the way Misha and Evelyn were acting. On his way out, he stopped by his sister. "Alexis, hit me up when you're done so I can scoop you. Be on point for your big brother, aight?" With the wink of an eye, he peeped the comprehension dawn on his baby sister's face.

Later on Alexis filled Franchize in on everything. She broke it all down. Misha owned Creations and was cool with mom before she passed. She was also cool with Negro's wife Kathy. She fronted like she wasn't interested until Evelyn started asking question. Then she put old girl to start working. It was hilarious the way these ladies were acting. Misha racked up a lot of points from what his sister told him. What topped it off was Alexis hooking her arm though his and saying, "She is wifey material. Trust me. I know." The subject got laid to rest, but Franchize started plotting on Miss Exotic.

CHAPTER 9

Blaze ended up in Auburn Correctional Facility. He sent Franchize a kite letting him know where he landed last week and he still hadn't received a reply. He knew it's a typical thing for a brother to go home and forget about the people locked up. He just couldn't believe Franchize would do what the average nigga does.

"Attention on the block, packages. Serrano..." Joey didn't hear anything after that. He couldn't believe he was being called for a package. Maybe real niggas do real things.

CHAPTER 10

Chino watched the money pour in. Lucking up with a new connect that has better work at cheaper prices. Just when things got good, an unexpected problem popped up. Everyone has Franchize's name in their mouths. Even the custies couldn't stop talking about him. The bozo wasn't even getting money and he took some of my shine. When the time is right…

CHAPTER 11

Franchize got to vibing with Misha. Evelyn kept throwing that thing his way, but he saw Misha as flawless. Many weeks passed and he finally arranged for a lunch date at Chipotle. They headed out of Creation and once in front, Misha spazzed out. She let the young boys know they had to move. Misha got heated noticing they were selling drugs in front of her place of business. Franchize kept quiet watching the scene play out before him.

"Hey big buns, calm the fuck down. My handle is Chino. Me and my team out here on this block now. It is what it is so don't stress yourself out and holla at a player." Chino looked at Franchize out of the corner of his eye waiting for a reaction. He hoped the bozo would play Captain Save-A-Hoe. "Chino, what's up baby bro? Let me holla at you on some

'G' shit for a second," Franchize suggested. Chino felt that he had Franchize right where he wanted him- four against one. He liked the odds. "Who you talking to bozo? You playing with my money?" Chino looked left then right at his boys.

Franchize noticed the little homies get tense and defensive. Too much experience under his belt told him what was about to go down. Knowing that the best defense is a great offense, he used his left hand to push Misha back while his right shot straight to Chino's nose. His hands went to his face, two of his homies stepped back, but the one standing to his right stepped forward. Franchize threw a left upper cut the youngster never saw coming. It connected with such force to his jaw that he was knocked out standing up. Franchize wasn't finished with him. The burning desire to send a message rove him forward to grip the back of the youngster's neck and jump with a knee aimed at his mouth. Teeth and blood exploded from his face. He fell limp to the floor. The other two cowards were walking backwards. Franchize punk faked the rush in their direction and they took off running.

Focusing back on Chino, a back hand brought him down to his knees. Misha became hysterical and Franchize had to give her the murder one look to quiet her and send chills down her spine. Chino's eyes cleared and he looked at Franchize with hatred. Franchize recognized the look and knew what it would bring. Nothing to be said. Nothing he could do to change the young man's choices. He kicked him in the chest and grabbed Misha by the arm. Pulling her into the street he hailed a cab and they got in.

CHAPTER 12

Chino got up and left his man. He went straight home. His big brother sat on the couch playing video games. He didn't notice his brother's condition as he went into the room. When he came out with a baby nine millimeter clutched in his hand and blood all over his face, his whole demeanor changed. Pappo jumped up from the couch and threw the remote on the floor. "Fuck happened to you? Spit it out. We riding on whoever together!" Pappo barked. "Franchize violated. Grip up big bro. We riding out."

"Hold up. I need you to sit down and put your pride aside for a minute". Pappo walked over and took the gun from Chino's hands. He tried to force him to understand who he was about to go up against. That's when it dawned on Chino that his brother was a coward. Telling him story after story about how dangerous Franchize had been wasn't helping the situation. He lost all respect for his brother. No matter who or what, nobody is above being laid to rest. Cleaning up, he figured he'd rock Franchize to sleep and pop his top after things calmed down.

CHAPTER 13

Gato had been a confidential informant for years. His contact Detective Rodriguez didn't like him but it didn't matter. Special Agent Blanche called the shots around here. When Blanche wanted something, he got it. This is why Detective Rodriguez didn't like him. Selling drugs and getting away with it was easy. Every time they tried to lock him up, Blanch would step in. He didn't know why the Special Agent went through so much trouble for him.

Word was he hated drug dealers, but Blanch tolerated him. If Blanche sent Detective Rodriguez to press him about Franchize that meant he wanted him to go down. Doing the right thing or not, he was going to take Franchize down to keep his own head above water and keep Blanch satisfied. It was time to go to work and earn his keep.

CHAPTER 14

Scrappy made it home and the only thing he planned to do was stay in his sister's crib until she got tired of him. Then he would start getting money. He didn't like being told that to do by his sister Evelyn and like the idea of being the man of the house. Lying back, he thought about the options available.

Nobody remembers or notices him. It's always like that. This time around he would make his way and leave a little splash in the water. Not too big of a splash because that would bring the sharks around and that had to be avoided. It felt good to be home and away from the dangers of prison life. Thinking about that time behind the rec. shack brought him shivers. Scrappy sparked a blunt to help him handle his demons.

CHAPTER 15

Franchize knew his older brother Negro could be defined as a square. It took all of his effort for him to have his big brother to keep up the membership at the local gym while he was locked up. Negro didn't like the shadiness because the membership is under a fake name. He did it out of love. Franchize told him to hold on to the key to the locker until the day he needed it.

Today Franchize came calling for the key. Negro knew the locker held a part of his brother that he prayed would stay buried. Negro took one look into those dark brown eyes and saw flashes of gunmetal grey appearing and vanishing like a ghost coming and going. He knew Franchize's actions spoke of a man doing his best to stay on the right path. All he could do short of denying his brother's request is talk some sense into him.

"My brother, you look a little on the edge. I don't know what you have in the locker, but it's a part of your past. It took you many years to get home and many months after that to get situated. I ask that you use your head in whatever you do. Put your faith in God. Stay on his path and all will be okay. I love you and need you. Having you work with me has been a blessing. I never thought I could teach you anything because you were always so smart and in the course of teaching you this trade, you have taught me what it feels like to be proud. For me, continue being the man you have become." Negro turned away and went back into his house.

Franchize stood there holding the key in his hand, turning it over with every thought. The genuine words his brother spoke made him feel a pang of envy for his ability to trust in putting everything in God's hands. In the life he lived, he knew he needed cold steel in his hands along with the Lord's blessings to make it out of the coming storm alive.

Franchize picked up the gym bag and every moment on the way home his nerves were on edge. Laying out $100,000 in hundred dollar bills, a .36 midnight special, a 21, and his pride and joy, a Colt .45 1911. He had three clips for the Glock and two for the .45. He laid the empty clips next to the two boxes of bullets he had for each gun. The last things he pulled out were his cleaning kit and knife. He needed to clean and oil his guns to prevent them from jamming when he needed them the most. The silencer almost didn't come off the Glock. When he did get it off, Franchize placed it next to the Glock's .9 mm hollow tips. The .45 had always been his favorite. It's beautiful, practical, dependable and strong. Tried and tested by the military for years, it sure is a dangerous one hitter quitter. The .38 midnight special came in a dull black to prevent reflections at night and didn't jam. It would have to be his go to workhorse if things heated up.

Franchize moved the bedside dresser and used the side of his Navy Seal ceramic switchblade to lift up the end of a loose floor board. Stashing 50 racks and the .38 with the rest of the bullets let him feel more comfortable executing his formulated plan. Putting the loaded handguns, extra clips, and 50 thousand in a book bag he called his uncle Tito. "Tito, what's up? Yeah, yeah, it's me... You've been waiting for my call? Yeah Tio, you got funny over the years I see. I need to check you. Is everything still good? Okay, I'm on my way. Same spot, right? Say no more."

CHAPTER 16

When it comes to having your hustle on lock, you could look at Tito as a prime example. He only dealt with stash boxes and whips. Never stepping out of his comfort zone, but mastering what he is good at. Not knowing how the future is to play out, Franchize needed to make sure he became prepared for anything. His mind kept flashing back to the day it all started. He couldn't believe three days had already past. On the cab ride back to Misha's crib, she flipped out over what happened. He wished he told her how he felt when she said she needed time alone to clear her head. It didn't matter now. He had business to handle. Looking up, he saw his uncle's used car dealership. He didn't believe they were at Northern Boulevard already. Paying the driver he hopped out.

Walking to the entrance of Tito's office he spotted some cars which peaked his interest. Stepping in, he greeted him. "Uncle Tito, it's good to see you healthy." Tito sharp as ever and in no mood for games or social calls which he knew this wouldn't be said. "My favorite nephew, what exactly brings you to my humble establishment?" Franchize knew what motivated his uncle and to avoid the bullshit, he pulled the 50 thousand out of the book bag and tossed it to him. "I'm looking to buy two cars."

Tito looked the money in his draw and laughed. "This would only get you one fairly new car equipped with the type of specification I remember you enjoying."

"I don't care about new or old. I want dependable with a high concentration of numbers and colors on the road like that green Camry and white Malibu you got out there with the spec you created for me, remember?"

"That's why people like us last nephew. All the flashy shit is a prison sentence waiting. I got a white Malibu, but the Camry for you is burgundy. There's been a lot of new technology since you went away. I can still handle the special specification, but this new stuff is truly expensive. Hydraulic lifts, separate compartments with independent power sources. Flawless symmetry in lines and high tech materials. Event the designs are unique for each model. Prices have gone way up for this type of equipment. Even if the police hit the car with an electrical surge, the stash won't open due to recent advancements. I'm going to take a loss giving you two cars with this new technology and the special specs you desire, but it's my present to you. Maybe you bring me some customers, maybe not. Let me show you how to activate everything. Also, if you want license plates activated for a year with all the paperwork, it's an additional $2,500 per car. All the paperwork for everything is included. I can give you plates until everything is ready. It's the best way to move and that money is still short for what you want, but I got you because you're family."

Franchize smiled. He knew the 50 thousand was more than enough to cover the costs. Tito wanted to make sure he got to keep every dollar that touched his hands. Some things never change. "I see things have improved since my last time here. You're a one stop shop now. I'm taking the Camry since it's got the specs I need. I will be back for the Malibu in 3 days. Have it ready or I'm going to take a refund. Now show me how it works." "Yeah nephew, no problem. I got you," Uncle Tito said wiping the sweat off of his forehead.

Franchize spent the next hour learning everything about his toy. It amazed him how far technology has come and its advantages were endless. He gave his uncle the Glock with the silencer to be put in the Malibu when it was ready. Pacing the blade and .45 in the Toyota's stash, he drove off plotting. He knew he didn't want to get back into the game, but his actions were saying otherwise. They could have stuck him in a time capsule forever and when he came out, he would still know the streets in and out. The game would always be filled with snitches, so it would only be a matter of time for a man's downfall. It also created a cycle of abuse and destruction in the community where his family lives. He knew Chino would end up becoming a problem and the way he would deal with it was against everything he was trying to stand for. Some things he couldn't control and the things he did he would have to act upon to start the journey toward the place he wanted to be. At the red light, he texted G Money for a meeting in Coney Island.

Franchize walked down the boardwalk towards G Money. He couldn't help feeling that old school brotherhood dies hard. They started a team coming up calling it 2.24. Two dons with 2 visions and 4 generals. He fell off the map when he went to prison. His mind started evolving and a bigger picture formed. He needed to make sure G Money understood he was out of the game. No more banging. He was trying to go legit.

Giving G Money a hug, Franchize said, "Ayo G, what's shaking bro? I see you're good and heard you're even better. We ain't really got to chop it up at my lil' get together when I came home. I give you my respect and love bringing news."

G Money got excited. "Bro, everything is good. The team has been waiting a long time for its fallen Don to touch the bricks. You know what's mine is yours and we got a mini empire. Two generals getting money hustling and two getting it the ski mask way. Their soldiers got loyalty pumping through their veins. When you come to sit at the table tonight, half the pot is yours. You could end up leaving with 12 or 14 stacks I know you need the money bro. The team also wants to pay their respects. You know what it is, two souls, one life to live."

Franchize let out a long breath that he held while G Money spoke. "G, I'm out. It's over for me. I'm trying to go straight. I got an issue or two I'm trying to handle myself, but I'm trying to lay to rest my inner Don. The team was the life to live coming up, but I changed bro. I want to try and make it the right way. It's all you now. With all my love and respect, I give you 2.2.4. Bro things…" "Fuck you talking about?" G Money barked. "You acting like this is an on and off switch. Oaths and pledges are to be stood by! 2.24 for life. Omerta. Am I my brother's keeper? Ride or die till the apocalypse. Niggas depending on you and you go jump in a square like it's all good!" G Money stood there letting the silence thicken, mean mugging Franchize. All of the love, loyalty, and respect he had within for Franchize started to change. Hatred, cruelty, and disgust started to brew underneath the surface. Looking to his left and the waves rolling in, he knew what must be done. The idea that formed became so clear, he smiled inwardly because he knew that this is what Franchize deserved. Hiding his true intentions he simply went back to talking to Franchize. "Fuck it bro. You're right. I just always thought we was gonna put that work in. Caught me off guard. My bad. Don't worry about shit. I got the wolves. Give them niggas a bonus on your behalf and find a way to put this extra bread to good use. Nigga can't really get too mad at extra money right?" G Money noticed Franchize begin to relax at his words. All he could think about was the mental chessboard that the set up mentally.

Franchize, surprised at his brother's change of heart, gave him a hug as he set off back to Queens. It turned out not to be as bad as it could've went. He knew the rules, the risks…

G Money watching Franchize pull off went over the oath they wrote years before. They all knew it by heart. It's part of the foundation.

Knowing that my brother's hand will lay my life to rest if I violate this pledge, I take the responsibility of 2.24 into my mind body and spirit. Our cause is greater than one man. United we stand against all odds. A Dons word is law. We lay to rest all obstacles in the way of 2.24. Our religion is money and we find all ways to get it. If a Don is to fall at the hands of another mad, he who makes vengeance reality will become the next Don with his vision etched in fire on the hearts of all 2.24. One Don makes two Generals. Two Generals make four Bosses. Four Bosses makes eight Soldiers. Our numbers are our strength.

G Money pulled out his phone and dialed his General. "Yo, we got an issue and you're going to love the way it's going to be handled. Let me give you the details…"

CHAPTER 17

"**M**isha, you been acting real stank the last couple of days. What's up with you? You caught Franchize with the next chic or something? You gots to lighten up because you are looking depressed," Evelyn said.

As Misha sat on Evelyn's futon sipping her drink, she thought about her homegirl's words and Franchize. She had too much going on right now to risk losing track of her priorities which were her business and its success. The way Franchize handled that situation angered her. He could've gotten both of them sent to prison or even killed by one of those young punks. She knew she sat on the fence with that to do about Franchize. "You know Eve, I think he might be keeping secrets because them dudes knew him. They called him Franchize and I didn't think nothing of it until now."

Scrappy fumbled the ice for the rinks he put together when he heard Misha say Franchize's name. Evelyn saw the look of shock on her baby brother's face and knew he was in the loop with some information. She wanted to bag Franchize badly and she needed her homegirl to get over him and fast. She need to get him alone to work her magic.

"Scrappy, why you looking like that? You know Franchize?" Evelyn asked. "Maybe." Scrappy looked at both women and became excited at their attention towards him. Evelyn pressed the issue. "What do you mean maybe? Scrappy, you better stop playing around and speak up. Or are you lying? Acting like you know someone to get into this conversation?" Eve know what she was doing. Scrappy had a complex about being called a liar and it wasn't right to play him like that, but she wanted to know anything about Franchize that her homegirl Misha didn't tell her.

"You talking about that big Spanish looking nigga that just came home?" Two heads nod yes at his words. "Yeah, son official. I was with him up top. He put that work in. Stabbing niggas up, moving that work, and they say he's a real murderer. He had the hood on lock before and now that he's home, N.Y. has its biggest problem walking around. I think he runs 2.24. Franchize is a true gangsta. You still think I don't know him?" Misha started crying and ran out of Evelyn's apartment. Scrappy looked at his sister confused. If Misha fucked with Franchize, why wasn't she happy she hooked up with a general? He knew he owed Franchize for saving his ass behind the wall and now he felt like he fucked up somehow. "Ayo sis, what's good with Misha? Why she acting like she caught the monster or something?"

"Baby bro, Misha don't want no hood nigga. Her pops died in prison. It took her a lot to even trust Franchize only to find he is exactly the opposite of what she wants in her life. She's a big girl and she will get over it. It's just going to take some time," Evelyn said. Scrappy understood, but at the same time he didn't. He thought all girls wanted gangsters in their lives. He figured he fucked up by talking too much. Misha is a fine shorty and if Franchize was trying to wife that, he didn't want the big guy to know he fucked that pack up.

Evelyn couldn't stop thinking about having sex with Franchize. She was going to do her best to lock him down. She did her homework and found out he didn't have any kids. If she had her way, it would be something that changed fast. Plotting, she thought about ways to get him alone.

CHAPTER 18

A week passed since he popped on Chino in front of Creations. Misha didn't call him back. Granted he only left one message, but he would get his manicure and see shorty. Parking the Malibu, he spotted Misha leaving. Franchize jumped out the whip and ran across the street. "Misha! Hold up. Let me talk to you for a minute."

Misha hesitated for a second then thought it best to get this out of the way now instead of dodging the issue. "Franchize, I'm sorry, but I can't do this anymore. I can't be with a gangsta. We both want to live in two different worlds and it's best if we went our own ways."

Franchize looked into Misha's eyes and said, "What two worlds are you talking about? There is only one world and we are both standing on it!

What's up with you? The road gets a little bumpy so you run? Or is it that you hate everything you don't understand? You're going to stand there and judge me without truly knowing all of me? The way I see it, you can't be with the man you love because I might break your heart. Without risks you're going to live a life without rewards. It's your life to live and you're the one that must live with the choices you make. I can't and won't force you to see our world as one. I love you, but I also see it's time I let go." Franchize spun off and jumped in his car. A couple of block later, stuck at a red light he noticed some clouds coming in casting a steel gray tint over his world. Confused by the raw emotions pumping through his veins, he felt that he just needed to be alone. So much to think about that the next several weeks passed in a blur.

CHAPTER 19

Misha wanted to fight with Franchize, curse him out and not talk to him at the same time. She was still tossing the words he said around in her head. She had to ask herself if he was any good for her. Men like that always lied and cheated. They didn't care if what they were doing broke hearts or destroyed lives. His words cut deep. They hurt and they felt like he had a look at her soul, reading aloud the exact passage she tried to hide even from herself. She got immersed in her work to the point of near exhaustion just to fall asleep. No matter how hard she tried to keep Franchize off her mind, she couldn't keep him out of her dreams. This was the type of distraction she tried to avoid from the beginning. How could she flush him from her system? She didn't have many days of resistance left in her if every day turned out the same without him.

Franchize started working overtime on the weekends and putting his all into his job. Even his brother Negro noticed the dedication. When his bosses called him in to speak of Franchize's accolades, his chest swelled with pride. It felt good hearing and seeing his brother's time spent in a positive place, but he could tell something was up with Franchize. Blowing off steam by drowning yourself in work is one thing, but to continue to do it for a long period of time couldn't be healthy. Negro didn't want Franchize burning himself out so he had to figure this out. At lunch Negro asked, "Franchize I see you're going through something. I know it's none of my business, but I want you to come to church with me on Sunday. Some food for the spirit. It may even put your problems into perspective." Franchize shook his head no before his brother even finished speaking. "Nah bro, I just need to work this out on my own. Let's get back to work."

Negro smiled at his brother "I thought I was the boss around here?" They both laughed heading back into the construction site. He felt the first surge of positivity in weeks. He appreciated his brother's genuine concern. Franchize even started recognizing his sister's attempts to put that upbeat positive energy into his life. Realizing he was the only one standing between himself and the life he waited so long to enjoy, he made a mental note to holla at Misha.

CHAPTER 20

Detective Rodriguez didn't like the way Special Agent Blanche came at him. The guy happened to be a real asshole. Now he was stuck with using his time and resources checking out Franklin Montenegro aka Franchize. Looking this guy's criminal history up led him to believe that he may be up to no good.

Detective Rodriguez grew up in the hood. He also despised people who didn't take all the opportunities this blessed country gave one to make it. He knew first hand that with some effort anyone could achieve the American dream. He grew up playing sports and studying hard. On his way through high school and college people always tried to get him to break the law and do things he wasn't supposed to do. He thanked God that he always took the time to think of the consequences of his actions.

He also knew he was lucky to be raised in a two parent household. His father was a good detective that retired with his mother in Florida. His father helped mold him, but he went to the same school and lived in the same neighborhoods as the criminals he chased. He didn't bother with petty crimes. He didn't want to hurt people's chances of making it. He only wanted the dangerous criminals and the ones who thought they could create an empire selling illegal drugs.

When his confidential informant came back saying Franchize didn't even smoke weed, the hairs on the back of his neck stood up. Gato was his best C.I. He would never risk his career to lock up an innocent man no matter from where the pressure came. He would fill out his reports and do some investigating. His gut feeling was that something big was in the air and it made his mind race. He didn't want to be anybody's scapegoat in a botched investigation. He remembered everything his father had told him about the FBI and not much of it was good. His instincts told him to start covering himself because things were getting too shady for his liking.

Detective Rodriguez started recording all conversation with Special Agent Blanche and with his C.I. Gato. He copied all of the documents pertaining to Montenegro that the agent produced and placed them in a safety deposit box his father kept at the local bank. He was taught you could never be too safe. Tonight he would tell his wife where to find answers if anything happened to him.

His wife Victoria always dismissed the idea or notion that anybody on the good side would do anything wrong. Being an Assistant D.A. she became more worried about him spending time on the streets she knew were violent. A couple more promotions and her husband would be safe behind a desk. She had a countdown for her husband. In three years he would have the position her family politicked for him to get. She came from a long line of lawyers and doctors. Her affluent family itched for her to join the private sector or the political arena. They couldn't stand that she married a police officer so they were going to make sure he had a respectable position to ease the sting. Her family loved to interfere with her career and with her private life. She was thankful her husband didn't mind the nudge her family would give his career. If he passed the tests, he should be given a fair shot.

This new development at work bothered her. She checked what her husband said with the D.A.'s office and nobody had heard regarding this investigation. It was time to let her office and parents involved to help her husband what was going on. She pulled out a bottle of wine and prepared dinner waiting for her husband to get off work.

CHAPTER 21

Evelyn got tired of her brother's antics. Every time she came back from work, she found a mess. Cleaning up after Scrappy got old quick. Those stank hoochie mamas he hung out with fouling up her apartment didn't help the situation either. Things were getting out o hand and she really wanted to have some alone time. She walked into the bathroom while Scrappy took a shower and squatted to pee.

"Ayo sis, you know I hate it when you come in here when I'm in the water. What's up with you?"

"Scrappy, I gots to pee and this is my house. Speaking of that, we need to have a talk."

"Eve, what do we need to talk about? You still trying to push that supermarket job on me knowing I ain't jacking it, I just came home and I gots to get prison out of my system."

"Baby bro, you only did two years and you've been home almost two months now. You haven't looked for a job and the supermarket is the best I can find for you. You're going to need to take it until you find something better. I rented you a room down the block and it's paid for the next two weeks. You start work tomorrow at 9 A.M. and I already called your P.O. and gave him the change of address. I can't keep holding your hand through life. If you want, you could always move in with mama in North Carolina."

"I see you have everything all figured out for me. I know when I'm being kicked out. Damn sis, I ain't expect you to do me like that. And you're flushing the toilet knowing the water gets COLD! You know what, I ain't even going to stress you. After I get dressed, show me my new crib. Does it have a T.V.?"

As Evelyn left the bathroom she said, "It has a bed, a closet, and a T.V. You're welcome by the way."

Finishing up the shower and moving in happened fast. His only thoughts were on how he would get money to pay for the room because he damn sure wasn't working for any supermarket. He knew he could do burglaries from time to time to keep his head above water. He got off light the last time and this time around he had the master plan. He figured he'd rob the niggas that were getting money so they wouldn't tell on what happen. He knew of a couple of dudes in the hood getting major money with easy to hit cribs. When Eve showed him his new apartment, he felt like he hit the lotto. Gato lived here and balling is what he do. He didn't think things could get any better until he noticed there was a fire escape outside the window. He felt good about the move now and didn't even care about the fake cool old head that turned out to be his roommate. He even had cable.

"Damn sis, you don't even have HBO," Scrappy said laughing.

"I see you're comfortable already. Call me if you need anything and if you get hungry you could always come and get a plate of food."

Evelyn walked out moving fast. She had her own plans to put in motion. She slipped Franchize's number off of Misha's phone and it was time to lay it down. He picked up on the second ring.

"Hello."

"It's Evelyn. How are you doing sweetie?"

"I'm good. Why; what's up?"

"Well, fuck it. Misha may be at my place around eight. It would be nice if you stopped by. You know where I live, right?"

"Yeah, over on 21st. I'll be there."

Evelyn even knew he liked Grey Goose and cranberry juice so she went to the liquor store and on the way back stopped to buy extra condoms to poke holes in with a needle.

She walked around the apartment with her sexiest lingerie beneath her bathrobe she booked from a hotel. The mood was set and excitement started to shoot through her body at the sound of a strong knock on her door. Opening it, she grinned like crazy at the look of surprise on Franchize's face as he assessed her assets through her loosely tied robe.

"Come on in," Evelyn purred as she grabbed his hand leading him to the couch. Franchize looked around absorbing his surroundings. Evelyn walked and came back with drinks in hand. "Good looking for the Goose and juice. What's up with Misha?" "She cancelled last minute. She didn't even know you were going to be here. No point in wasting a bottle of Goose. Why don't you get comfortable and take those boots off?"

Franchize's mind started racing. Pieces of the puzzle started to fall into place. His options sprung to life amongst another thing. Evelyn was bad. A real pretty shorty and crazy thick in all the right places. A serious wagon with perfect sized breasts. A slim waist and a pair of juicy lips with chinky eyes made her almost irresistible.

Evelyn noticed the bulge in Franchize's pants as he leaned back. She undid her robe and let it drop around her ankles. She turned around and bent at the waist to pick it up. Franchize could see everything through the sheer fabric as her basketball sized ass cheeks jiggled. The primal urge to get up and fuck her crazy right there surged through his nervous system making his dick twitch She lingered a moment longer than necessary bent over then placed the robe on the coffee table as she sat down next to him. She ran her hand down his chest, over his abs on her way to his manhood. His dick begged to be released as it strained against his jeans.

When she placed her hand on his belt buckle, she was surprised to find his hand on top of hers. He looked her right in the eyes she could see the lust brewing in him. His tense muscles were giving off a heat that made her pussy wet. Then he surprised her. He got up and tuned to face her. The spring board on his pants was at eye level now and she could feel her mouth start to water when he dropped the bomb. She couldn't believe what she was hearing. Never before in her life. She felt numb as the weight of his words crushed her.

"Ayo Eve, that's a slimy ulterior motive you used when you asked me to come over. You're sexy as fuck and you can see I'm barely holding myself together, but I see I have to think for both of us. What about Misha? You know I got it bad for shorty. Even as crazy as I'm feeling right now, what we were about to do would scar baby girl forever. You're her best friend and even if she doesn't know it yet, I'm her future husband. People may call me a gangsta, but I know how to be a gentleman. Let's act like this never happened and work with each other to make Misha happy. You're beautiful, Eve. Don't you ever forget that. Shhh, don't say a word." Franchize bent forward and gave her a tender lingering kiss on her cheek that was so close to her lips a tingling feeling shot all over her skin and melted away the rage that built up.

As she watched him walk out, it dawned on her that he is the real deal. Misha happened to be the luckiest woman alive and she didn't even know it. Evelyn felt embarrassed at the way she acted. She knew she had to make it up to Misha or she wouldn't be able to live with herself. She was so frustrated that she went to her bedroom and pulled out her toys. She needed to release the tension that had built up by her pelvis. If she couldn't have the real deal, the next best thing would definitely do the trick. Franchize may be out of bounds physically, but he damn sure wasn't mentally. It was time to get frisky.

CHAPTER 22

P lotting to catch Franchize slipping was in the works. He got Franchize's routine down and now he had the drop on this bozo.

Chino sat on the bumper of an old car in the cut. He pulled out his coke and used his key to take a couple of more sniffs. He loved being wired. He felt it made him sharper when putting in work. His heart had started racing faster when Franchize walked out of the building. Franchize looked in every direction but his.

Waiting for Franchize to clear the van that blocked a clear shot, he cocked his .380. At the first sign of a shadow coming past, he let loose. The first bullet hit the van by Franchize's head and he kept letting that .380 bark. Chino shot off the whole clip. His palms were sweaty and he held the gun in a death grip. He wanted to make sure Franchize got hit and was dead so he moved forward past a couple of cars. He was nowhere in sight. Chino looked underneath the van and his mouth went dry when he didn't see Franchize.

Franchize reacted as soon as he heard the cocking sound of the gun. He knew what it was and got low using cars as cover until he made it to the Malibu. Throwing the key in the ignition and hitting the code with practiced efficiency a lifetime of heartbeats passed as he watched the stash open up. He grabbed the already loaded .45, cocked with one in the head and the safety off. He saw Chino make his way past the van and Franchize let thunder strike. The side mirror next to Chino exploded.

Chino tried to fire back but all he got were the clicks of an empty gun. Panicking at the danger at hand, he ran for it jumping the little fence that enclosed the parking lot.

Franchize had the open shot as soon as Chino started running but he didn't take it. He promised himself when he was up north that he would do his best to avoid killing anybody ever again on impulse. That's how he got knocked the first time ad he learned from his mistakes. It's something he took serious.

Franchize picked up the shell casing to the bullet he let off before jumping in his car putting everything back in the stash and driving off.

The kid fucked up and now he was as good as dead. He should have worn a mask. Turning the corner, Franchize noticed the cop cars speeding in his direction towards the scene. All thoughts of Chino disappeared as he analyzed the situation. He couldn't afford being pulled over right now and his response time has improved over the years. After the cop cars passed, he breathed easy. At the rate things would be picking up, he would have the pulse of the city down pact again in no time.

Chino made it to his crib and put the .380 up after he reloaded it. He knew it was war now. Just how bad was it? Why didn't Franchize get scared and run like everyone when he heard the shots? Motherfucker shot back!

Chino's mind weighed out what happened. He knew that if you shot a fake gangsta, they never came back to the hood. The few who did changed their lives or took a shot or two back before giving up and moving on. Franchize must think this the movies or something acting like an action hero. Chino didn't like the way shit went down. He figured he would lay low for a couple of weeks then take a couple of more shots at Franchize if he stood in the hood. Soon it would be time to turn it up.

~ ~ ~

Special Agent Blanche took a vacation from work to handle a couple of things and visit his wife Mary and his daughter's grave site. He missed his wife Mary and daughter Ashly deeply.

Standing in front of Ashly's grave, Special Agent Blanche lost it.

"Baby, I swear to you that I will make Franklin Montenegro pay for ruining our lives. You would still be here by my side if that scumbag didn't trick you into smoking that pot cigar laced with crack. I will get him. I promise you".

It still drove Agent Blanche crazy when he thought about what Franchize did. The scumbag and his crew went around giving away pot cigars laced with crack whenever they wanted new customers. His daughter admitted to only wanting to smoke weed once in a while, but she couldn't stop smoking crack. Franchize destroyed countless lives, all for the bottom line. A whole neighborhood thrown into chaos just to line his pockets with the hurt and pain of families dealing with a newly addicted loved one.

No matter how many rehabs he forced Ashly into, she always relapsed when she got out. The stealing got out of hand and desperate to help her, he kicked her out hoping tough love would help. After she stole Mary's wedding band when she came to visit, she was never allowed back into the house. Mary died giving birth to Ashly and he tried his best as a single parent only to have the brightest spot in his life snuffed out.

He found her two years later strangled to death in a hotel room. She lived as a prostitute selling herself to get high. He caught the sick fuck that killed his baby, but deep down he still felt that Franchize was responsible for everything. He would make sure Franchize paid for stealing the potential his little girl's life promised. It was time to put more pressure on Detective Rodriguez for a bust while he worked the other angles.

~ ~ ~

Linda Johnson was a hard working single mother with an extensive caseload at the Queens Parole Office. She has one son in LaGuardia Community College and another at Rikers Island Correctional Facility for drug possession. A sample of both worlds gave her insight working with parolee's. She knew the good and the potential these convicts had if they got themselves together. She also had no problem violating a parolee if they played games or if she thought they were getting out of line. She had a duty to protect society by making sure her parolees did the right thing. Her job was simple but tedious. She divided her parolee's into 3 categories above and beyond what her office standards were. She has done this job for 20 years already and became knowledgeable of all its aspects. Linda set her parolees into High Risk, Medium and Low Risk according to her standards after all the tags and suggestions that came along with the file. Her intuition had a higher accuracy rate than all of the squares her parolees were supposed to fit into. The an FBI agent walked into her office. She knew nothing good would come of this so she got out her paperwork to start the process of a violation.

After brief pleasantries, things weren't clicking. For once, she studied Franklin Montenegro's file for months. She talked to his family members. Popped up at his job and apartment at various hours to make sure he wasn't slipping through the cracks. Two, he made more money than she did and lived modestly. No flashy clothes or jewels. Simple furniture and living arrangements. She even drug tested him more than most and called him in at the last minute from time to time to see if he was slipping , but he was always clean. Last but not least, she could read people and Mr. Montenegro is as genuine as they come. She usually didn't put people in the low category that had a manslaughter charge this fast, but he earned it along with a grain of her trust with his hard work. Linda never took things at face value so it was time to investigate a little further with some questions of her own.

"Mr. Blanche, why exactly do you want me to violate the parolee in question?"

"Ms. Johnson, that is confidential at this time. We just need your office to cooperate with ours."

"Mr. Blanche, you have to realize that I have to put something down on this paperwork as the reason."

"May I call you Linda?" Blanch asked.

"No."

"Okay, why don't you use one of the minor infractions he has broken and violate him on that?"

"Why Agent Blanche, I would have already done that, but Mr. Montenegro doesn't have any minor or major violations at hand to leverage against him. So why don't you give me some more information so I can make an informed decision as to what I'm about to do."

"I'm sorry Mr. Johnson, it doesn't work like that. Why don't you just violate him? You know your job better than I do and I know from experience that you could make something stick if you wanted it to."

"Well I'm sorry Mr. Blanche, it doesn't work like that. This would be a breech in protocol on my part to falsify a government document and give my bosses ammunition to fire me if this was to blow up in my face. If you can't give me any information as to why I should violate Mr. Montenegro, I'm not going to be able to help you."

"Ms. Johnson, I'm truly disappointed in your decision. I would appreciate it if you could let me have a copy of Mr. Montenegro's file before I take my leave."

"Umm, sure," she said.

Handing Agent Blanche the copy brought up a strong sense of bullshit coming from his direction. A field agent almost never came in. usually a call would be made to her boss's boss and all types of crap would roll downhill with the forms dilled out on all the reasons for the parolee's violation. She made a mental note to verify this agent's presence and story. He looked weird. Her intuition got her over a lot of rough situations before and it screamed for her to add this task to her to do list before she left the office for the day.

Agent Blanche was infuriated with Linda Johnson's actions. No one ever sticks up for a convict, especially in law enforcement. It's unheard of. The natural laws of people and this world were acting up. One thing was for certain, the law of average would level out sooner or later. So Franchize made a lot of money legally. Well that will change after his visit to Franchize's bosses and some badge flashing. Killing his income should throw him off balance for some. The master stroke of his plan would come later. First he needed to place a chink in this scumbag's armor so everything would be more plausible when it all came together. If both easy ways to take Franchize down were out of the questions, the extremely illegal way was available. Detective Rodriguez and his confidential information couldn't perform on a simple task and this convict lover Linda Johnson was blinded by a fake persona being put forward by a scumbag. Franchize will pay and he will feel the hurt and pain forever.

CHAPTER 23

Negro was frustrated by the call he got from his boss. For no exact reason, he now had to fire his own brother. It didn't seem fair. Now that he had his brother in front of him the gravity of what could happen had Negro grabbing at straws. Not wanting to lie to his brother, he told him the truth.

"Franchize, the company decided to let you go. I don't know what happened, but it doesn't matter. To hell with them. You know I got a side business doing the same thing we do here. I've never paid it the right amount of attention, but if you want, you could take it over and run it. Work onsite with the established crew so you learn on the fly. You would be your own boss and make about the same you do here. You're my brother. If you can commit to running and working there as hard as you have here, I would make you my partner by giving you 50 percent of the business. Call it incentive to make it grow. You know I got a wife and kids so I need the benefits of this job here and wifey would go crazy if I pursued my dream. What do you say?"

"I don't know bug bro. How about you give me three weeks personal time? With that I can say I'm most likely to jump on it fully. I just need some time to recharge for this pivot," Franchize said. Getting up, he gave his brother a hug and walked out of his office.

Negro felt the aura of danger radiating off of his brother and would have giving him more just to see him stay on the right path. For some reason unknown, forces were pulling him in a direction where chaos reigned supreme. Something was going to tip Franchize in one direction or the other. All he could do was his best to push Franchize down the right path and pray.

Franchize went to go see one of his boys that he could count on from the network he established before he went to prison. Billy was cool and he owed Franchize. One night many years ago, some thugs from the hood tried to rob Billy. What stood out to Franchize is that Billy wasn't going for it. Billy asked the stick up crew, "Hey, ay of you got a gun? If you don't we are going to have to fight! The only way you're going to get mines is after you knock me out". Right after he said that, the trio was on him, ping ponging Billy half way down the block. Franchize was in the cut and observed everything. He didn't like civilians getting got because it brought heat to the blocks where money was being made. The display of heart helped Franchize make his decision.

Stepping out from the dark doorway, he punched one of the attackers in the back of the head. He fell on his face out cold and Franchize moved on stabbing the other man that was only focused on jumping Billy. Franchize watched him spring into the air at the feel of the knife. Once the man's feet touched concrete again, he was off to the races. The last thug was trying to figure out what was happening when he looked around. Billy's left hooks and straight rights rained on the poor guy until he hit the floor. Billy gave him two swift kicks for good measure when they heard the sirens in the background. Billy saw the hesitation in Franchize's movements and said, "My building is the next one over. We could hide out until the coast clears. You drink?"

Franchize became intrigued with the way Billy acted and said, "Sure, let's go." He wanted to find out what Billy was about. After introductions, Billy passed him a Heineken and make sure Franchize knew to keep it down so his wife and daughter could sleep. He had an 8 year old baby girl and had been married for 9 years back then. He was the manager of a local factory where they made metal chains. Franchize was truly interested in what Billy had to say. He learned a lot from the man that night. He even learned that Billy was broke when he emptied his pockets on the table top. A couple of crinkled dollar bills and some change was all he had. Franchize couldn't help himself and started laughing. He watched as Billy put the money into a pink piggy bank.

"This is my daughter's college fund." A newfound respect formed for Billy. Money wasn't a thing for Franchize at that time and thinking quickly Franchize asked, "What would these acid baths for the chains dissolve? Hypothetically, if a dog was thrown into one, what would be left?"

"Well if you didn't take it right out and left it in there, nothing would be left. It's industrial strength acid. The chains are run through it to clean them after they are formed. Even the metal isn't allowed to sit in the acid baths. Why do you ask?"

"What if I was to say that I had $75,000 for your daughter's college fund to use that acid bath once in a while?"

"I would've done it for free after what you did for me tonight. Do you need me to go with you when you're using it?"

"No, I just need you to show me how to use it safely so I don't cook myself. After that, I'm just going to need to borrow the keys from time to time. Are there any cameras?"

"No, it's old school. Not even a security guard. Nobody wants to steal heavy chains for some reason."

"Good, I will be back in an hour with that $75,000."

When Franchize walked out, Billy's wife came out of the bedroom and asked, "Who was that?" Billy looked her in the eyes and said, "Jessica, he is a fallen angel. Now go back to sleep and I will be with you later".

After that night many years ago, Billy became a close friend. When he saw his boy with bunches of gray streaking through his hair, Franchize couldn't help teasing him. "Hey old man! If you had to choose between a walker and a retirement home, which would it be?" Billy laughed at Franchize's shot.

"You don't look so young yourself. How have you been?" Billy asked.

"How's the wife and the baby girl Angela doing?"

"They are great. Angela goes to M.I.T and has a 3.8 GPA. Wants to be some kind of computer software engineer or something."

"Daddy's baby girl making him proud. It's truly a blessing."

"We should all get together for dinner sometime. The wife makes a killer pot roast."

"Sure, that sounds great. Also, I may need to use the factory sooner or later. I just need to know if we still good?"

"You know better than that Franchize. I am even willing to help with anything if you need an extra hand," Billy said.

"Nah nah Billy, I wouldn't feel comfortable anyway. I just needed to know that you would produce. Keep your cell on at night just in case."

"Alright Franchize. I'm here for you any time. See you around. Stay safe kiddo."

CHAPTER 24

Something is always right around the corner to drag you down. The man that's prepared that can hurdle obstacles. All the years spent in prison thinking of every possible contingency plan possible made Franchize grunt. He committed them to memory so when the expected action occurred, the reaction would be automatic. He knew hesitation creates devastation. Every road he traveled had to be a two way street in his life. Franchize understood what needed to be done. The consequences were real. Some people talked a good one. But that's it. All they did was talk.

Real killers moved in silence. Once a real killer's mind is made up, a plan of action unfolds. Society doesn't think murder is right, but when your gut tells you *this needs to be done*, what do you do? There are different rules for different circles. In the end it all comes down to the most basic form of animal instinct- survival. The need to live triggers things in us that we did not know exist. Franchize knew another prison sentence would be his death. Whoever creates the possibility of him going back would become a casualty of war. He hoped things could get done the way he had planned. If not, he was prepared to hold court in the streets of New York.

Franchize noticed his phone ringing so he turned down the throw back Jeezy.

"Speak on it."

"We need to talk," Misha said.

"You calling shots now?"

"Franchize, please, don't be difficult. You got time?"

"Give me 15, your place."

Franchize turned down 21st street and stomped on the gas.

~ ~ ~

Scrappy climbed down his fire escape making his way to Gato's apartment. With a stroke of luck, the money getter lived two floors down. Scrappy plotted for the last couple of days and this Friday night would be the best time to hit his crib. Scrappy felt confident in his all black outfit with the skin tight latex gloves he learned about in prison. He tried the window and to his surprise, it flew it flew open. All Scrappy could do was grin as he hopped inside.

Scrappy went straight into the bedroom. He started with the dresser's bottom drawer. This way he didn't have to close them to see into the next drawer. Finding money and jewels made Scrappy jump. His book bag was almost filled as he made his way to the closet. That's when thing started to get weird. He opened up a suitcase to find a note saying "Property of the NYPD". There were labels of cameras, microphones, and receivers. They were small so you couldn't tell if someone was wearing them, but what were they doing in Gato's crib? This nigga had to be working for police.

Getting back to the search, he found a 9 mm under the mattress. Walking into the living room froze him in his tracks. He realized that the walls were covered in charts detailing the who's who in the hood. The other bedroom was even worse. It was his office. This shit was bad. A computer table off to one corner had a bunch of a machines around it. On the walls there were more charts, but these had memory sticks in slots next to the pictures. Scrappy went straight for the closet. He found a couple of thousand more on the top of the door frame and a small fire proof safe under some clothes in the cut. His book bag was full so he grabbed a canvas bag when a thought hit him. He took all the memory sticks from the wall and the brain of the computer. He snatched up the lab top with that filling his canvas bag.

Scrappy struggled with his load the two floors up the fire escape. Once inside his room he counted out $48,400. His biggest come up ever. He thought about the money he could get from Franchize for the memory stick of info he had snatched from Gato.

He also wanted to know what was in the little fire proof safe. He saw it had a flimsy lock so he got to work. Inside he found 600 grams of cocaine, a digital scale and some baggies. Jackpot. Now he really needed to get rid of Gato. The schemes playing out in his mind all led him straight to Franchize. With what he was thinking, only Franchize would pay him and take care of Gato at the same time. It was the only win-win scenario they could come up with. He needed to make sure he painted Gato as a real threat to Franchize. That would allow him to move Gato's coke without its owner looking for it. He would have to sit on the jewels for a while, but he just couldn't sit still. He made up his mind, and thought it better to see Franchize now to try and convince him to handle Gato ASAP. He wanted to make it look like he was returning a favor, but getting what he wanted instead. Scrappy thought it was time to go chill in front of Franchize's crib.

CHAPTER 25

"**M**isha- what's up? You called me over and now you're all quiet. I don't read minds so speak up, "Franchize demanded.

"There is no rush for what I have to say Franchize. I just needed to look at while I made up my mind. I need to feel secure in knowing that you're not a gangsta trying to take over New York City. I need to be sure you won't leave me for a life in prison. There is so much I need and I don't know if you're ready."

Misha broke eye contact and looked down. Franchize walked over and cuffed her beneath the chin, tilting her head so she could see directly into his eyes and said, "I don't want to run N.Y. and I'm not going to prison. I am who I am doing what I can. What you see is what you're getting. As for the things you need to know, you're going to have to bide your time with me to find out in time. In time, you will be secure and learn to trust me. All I can prove to you at this moment is that I love you."

Franchize's lips raced towards hers in a wave full of passion. He pulled her into him and felt her melt in his arms. All the resistance she was trying to expel dissipated. Franchize wasn't in the mood to play around. They undressed each other with urgent energy pulsing through their veins. He picked her up by her ass cheeks and moved her to the bed. He could feel the heat of her sex on his body. He kissed her neck on his way down. He popped one breast out by pulling on her bursting bra with his teeth. As he played with the side of her breast with his lips and tongue, his hand scooped out her other sexy mound. He kissed around the edges of her nipple then brought her breasts together. Once her hard peaks touched, he covered them with his lips and continued caressing them with his tongue. Splitting and circling them until he heard her moan. Franchize kissed his way to her belly button. He paused giving it a second of his attention then continued his way to the heat that drew his focus. When he got there, he lifted her legs over his shoulders. He kissed her thighs, bit them, licked them and rubbed his beard all over the inside of her thighs feeling the heat of her sex drifting up. He felt her body tense as she grinded her hips towards his face. His grip around her thighs didn't let her get far, His dick was rock solid and throbbed at her every movement. He breathed heavy gasps of hot air through his mouth knowing the rushes of air hit her pussy. He was amazed at how her clit swelled and that shit dripped. His mouth became watery watching the exotic beauty squirm beneath him. She drove him crazy and he started to eat. The more he ate her out, the more he got turned on. When he felt that first tremble through her body, he knew she was ready.

Stopping, Franchize stood up with his erection standing at full attention. Guiding her off the bed, Misha stumbled onto her knees. She took him whole on the first pull into her mouth. She sucked like a mad woman. Her moaning caused a vibrating sensation up and down his length as she worked him like a pro. He knew he couldn't take much more of this so he grabbed her by the back of her head and pulled his dick out of her mouth and rubbed it across her face and over her lips.

Lifting her up on shaky legs, he bent her over the corner of the bed. Once his tip slid into the juicy heat of her sex, he grabbed hold of both hips. He pumped half strokes into her until he was thrusting his whole length deep and hard into her. She gasped and moaned with every thrust, but he was just getting started and frustration was a motherfucker. He pounded her pussy trying to get lost in its glory. He felt her cumming on his dick. Her legs shook and twitched ready to give out on her, but he didn't want to bust just yet. Pulling out he flipped her onto her back on the bed. He ate her pussy some more until the urge to bust calmed down. Shifting her to the middle of the bed, he climbed on top of her. They were eye to eye when his dick found her flowing juices telling him it was time to slip and slide.

He fucked her with all of the conflicting emotions he had inside of him. He pulled her hair and grabbed her face. She wrapped her legs around him, throwing the pussy into his thrusts. Her moans turned into screams. He couldn't take it anymore. He felt himself ready to cum and tried to pull out. Misha's legs wrapped around him, enticing him deeper into her. Losing control, Franchize exploded with all the backed up tension he had deep inside of her. He could feel the second and third jet streams shoot into her.

By the time Misha realized what had happened, she was too exhausted to mentally struggle with the possibilities and consequences of what this might bring. All she wanted was to be wrapped in Franchize's strong arms. As she drifted off to sleep, Franchize's mind raced. He couldn't lay still and decided to take a drive to relax and think.

CHAPTER 26

He drove around the neighborhood working things out his mind. His family gave an endorsement and that was big. He knew Misha had her head in the place and independence radiated in her action. She was thick and sexy. To top it all off, she wanted the best for him and not the glamorous lifestyle he could create if he slipped back into the game. She wasn't only good girl, but a go getter. He could tell she had him sprung. That good-good had his nose wide open. He had to chill and be easy. If not, she would have him hooked then cooked. He felt she could be his ride or die. He just didn't want to fall into a trap. His best option would be to watch her walk into the role she wanted to play in his life. It would be the only to truly know where she belonged. I didn't make sense to try to figure out the most complex species in this world. All he needed for now was what he saw in her- a sincere and genuine woman. Time would tell if she was right for him. Time always does.

With the music bumping and his thoughts stuck on shorty, Franchize almost didn't notice Chino sitting on a project bench with Gato. He looked around and felt it was a good night to test a theory. Turning down 26th Road, he made the call to Billy. He was downstairs waiting when Franchize pulled up. With the window down, Billy passed Franchize the keys and gave him a pound at the same time. Franchize kept it moving on his way home to change cars and clothes. What he found waiting for him was a surprise. Son looked familiar. When he explained who he was and that he had some info that really needed his attention, Franchize knew it was imperative to give him a minute to break it down.

If what Scrappy was saying rang true, then he was in some trouble. The implications of what Gato up to were infuriating. Playing with a man's freedom on some snitch shit is something you don't do. He felt like they wanted him to come out of retirement to put them into permanent one. "Ayo Scrappy, give me two minutes and then we're rolling, ya dig?"

Franchize changed clothes and grabbed a duffel bag from his sister's crib with some things he might need. It was two in the morning and she woke up when she heard him moving around. "Oh shit, baby sis; you scared the shit out of me! What you doing up?"

"How could I sleep with all the noise you make coming downstairs? What are you doing with that bag? Don't act like I don't know what's in it."

"Alexis, don't worry. Take my phone and call or text every 15 minutes until I get back, okay?"

"Yea. Just be safe. I will be worried until you get back," Alexis said.

Franchize gave her a kiss on the cheek and kept it pushing. "Ayo Scrappy, follow me." Franchize led the way to the white Malibu across the street. It made Franchize feel a little bit better noticing no one was really outside when he left with Scrappy. As he drove, the little guy kept talking about Gato and what he had found.

"Yo Franchize, I'm telling you someone needs to ride on Gato and fast. Let him know shit is real. Now that I think about it, I'm gonna need some lay low cash and I'm broke. This way I can make sure the info I grabbed up finds its way to the bottom of the river without any worries. You know what I mean?" Scrappy said.

Franchize knew exactly what Scrappy meant. "Lil bro, don't stress that. Once this Gato situation is cleared up, I got you with 5 stacks. Just ride with me. Be easy lil bro, I got you," Franchize said. Scrappy felt his master plan coming together and it was like hitting the lotto with money pouring in from every angle.

Franchize pulled up on Gato and Chino and sat back to get the tempo of the streets into his veins. Once comfortable, he hit his code to pull out the Glock and silencer. He checked the clip and made sure there was one in the head. He was about 15 yards from his targets, but this was risky part. "*No wasted movements*," he thought as he opened the door. He moved with purpose but not running. He walked up on Gato and Chino before they even noticed what was happening. The weed and liquor buzz they had died as they saw Franchize standing in front of them holding a mean machine. They tried to hold up their hands, but Franchize barked two orders in an authoritative voice that said "I'm not playing".

"Hands down; walk that way."

"Ayo Franchize, fuck this about bro?" Gato asked.

"Just keep it moving and jump in the back seat," Franchize ordered.

They were at the car in no time. Franchize noticed the look on Chino's face. He knew the lame was about to make a run for it. Once Gato opened the door, Franchize shot Chino in the head,

"What the fuck! Yo, you crazy," Gato squealed.

"Shut up. Pull him in or I'm shooting you too."

Gato pulled Chino's Corpse into the back seat next to him. He was stretching Chino's body across his lap when Franchize bent forward and shot Gato in the head too. No way was he going to drive with a scared rat behind him. Closing the door, he walked to the driver's side and jumped in. Taking off nice and easy, he noticed looked pale. "Yeah, shit just got real," Franchize said. There was no way he was letting Scrappy out of his sight now.

He got to the factory in quickly. Once the gate was open, he could drive onto the factory floor. He took the keys out the ignition in case Scrappy got any ideas and opened up shop. Franchize didn't plan on staying long. Popping the trunk, he grabbed the duffel bag. Opening it up, he pulled out a heavy plastic tarp. Spreading it on the floor was the easy part. Now, he had to get the bodies on it.

"Ayo Scrappy, you ain't gonna earn your 5 stacks just sitting in the whip. You gots to put some work in so get out here."

Scrappy caught an STD fucking around tonight. He truly was Scared to Death. He couldn't even make eye contact with Franchize. "Help me get their clothes off, " Franchize ordered. Working together, they prepped the bodies in a flash. There wasn't even that much blood. The silencer on the Glock the 9 mm shell enough to stay inside of their heads. Therefore, the bullet holes barely leaked. Goes to show you Hollywood don't know shit Franchize thought.

He got the duct tape out of the bag and grabbed the remote to the big chain with hooks. Franchize maneuvered it until the chain came down over the tarp. Once in place he duct-taped Gato first, then Chino to the steel hook. Flipping the other switch, the lid to the acid bath chamber opened up. Using the remote, he directed the bodies over the acid and lowered them.

Scrappy was so fixated on what was going on that he never saw it coming. Franchize shot him in the back of the head. There was no point in letting this rat walk off without the possibility of parole Franchize rationalized. He remembered Scrappy snitching behind the rec shack in the yard when they were locked up and felt that type of behavior only repeated itself. Taking Scrappy's clothes off, he found his keys. Little man talked too much and he told Franchize like 5 times where he stashed everything. It was all under his bed in his new apartment. He has a roommate but from what Franchize understood, the old head could sleep through a storm. He felt it was wonderful to just listen sometimes. That would be his last stop on his way to dump the whip and hammer.

He put all the clothes in the duffel bag and brought the chain back with the remote, Franchize felt secured when he saw the hook had nothing on it. He threw the duffel in the trunk and finished his business with Scrappy. Going through Scrappy's room surprised Franchize in many ways. Little man didn't say anything about the money and coke he found. It was an added bonus, but the jewels could stay. Grabbing up the coke and memory sticks, Franchize continued his mission.

Downstairs he got on a payphone and called his sister's cell phone. "Alexis, grab my whip and meet me by Con Ed. The second parking lot from 21st Street. Wait for me on the side street. Five minutes good? Okay, leave our phones in the crib sis. Everything's good. Just be there."

On the way to the spot, Franchize drove down Shore Boulevard. Stopping, he got out and tossed the Glock in the east River. In the parking lot, Franchize put together his spoils of war with the unused tools into a different bag. He took two gas canisters he always kept full out of the trunk and poured them all over the interior. The Malibu and the Camry had been equipped with special modifications. They had enough explosives to make a suicide bomber proud. The extra gas was to make sure the crime scene investigators didn't get shit. Hitting a different code, he set a timer of 3 minutes. His sis had already pulled up so he walked bag in hand, with measured steps, trying not to draw attention. Jumping in, he spoke calmly to Alexis. "Pull off nice and easy and take us home." She didn't say a word when he hit his code and .45 came into sight. He put the coke in the compartment next to it. He knew the money wouldn't fit and put it in his sister's lap. "Keep the money Alexis. I don't need it," Franchize said as an explosion reverberated through windows even though they were several blocks from the parking lot. Franchize didn't even blink as Alexis flinched.

"I need my phone and a shower. I'm gonna leave this outfit at your crib. Wash it tomorrow and donate it or something."

"Franchize, when is all this madness going to end? I ask Pistol the same thing. That explosion still has my pulse racing. I don't care what it was about. I don't even want to know. You know I got your back no matter what. You're my brother and I love you. You just have to try and do things differently. Everything like this won't always be alright. You spent a lot of years learning that fact first hand. Don't become a statistic with recidivism. You're 31 and don't even have a kid. Settle down. Misha is good for you and that's where you should be focusing your attention. Please big bro, do it for me."

"I got you sis and I know you're right about Misha. I'm working everything out. Just give me some time. I promise this will all be over soon. We good?" Franchize

"You know are. Now, hurry up, I want to go to sleep."

CHAPTER 27

Being exhausted did not mean he didn't have to take care of his responsibilities. The sun had come up and Franchize knew Billy must need his keys. Looking at the clock, he calculated he had an hour. Franchize couldn't resist the temptation of a good cup of coffee.

He felt that there was nothing like some gasoline to keep the engine running. Black with no sugar is how he drank it. Halfway through his extra strong brew, a knock sounded on his door. Without hesitation, he picked his phone and tapped the options to look through the security he had in the hallway. It was his P.O. Ms. Johnson. Looking around, Franchize made sure there weren't any violations lying around. She knocked harder and he had to take deep breaths to ease the panic that tried to build within him. He started to feel confident everything was in order. Time to work his magic.

"Ms. Johnson, how good to see you. Please come in. Would you like a cup of coffee?"

"I'm sure you're happy to see me Mr. Montenegro. Are you alone or do you have guests? "

"I'm alone ma'am. May I get you that cup?"

"No no; I'm good. I'm fine looking around. I see you're really organized. You have this weekend off, but your bed is already made? Are you just coming in or going out?"

"I had some weekends off but that's something I wanted to talk to you about. For some reason, the suits at headquarters decided to let me go. I have some very interesting questions to ask you."

Ms. Johnson's memory flashed to Special Agent Blanche's face and thought it might have been a bad idea to give him Mr. Montenegro's file. She didn't believe in coincidences especially since her friend at the agency told her Agent Blanche was on vacation. Playing her cards close to her chest so Mr. Montenegro stayed on a need to know basis, she asked him, "So what's interesting?"

"Well being fired might be a blessing or a curse depending on how you look at it. My brother has given me 50 percent ownership of a construction company he started years ago to supplement his income. If I am allowed to become self-employed, I will be able to make about the same amount of money, but have to work more hours. The possibilities are endless, but

I don't know parole protocol so it's a blessing expert stopped by."

"Mr. Montenegro, everything is going to have to be on the level. Documentation of you being a partner and of how you're paying yourself. Addresses of where your office is located and what site you're working on will always have to be current. All licenses will need to be up to date. I don't think I left anything out but how serious are you about this?"

"Extremely. Success isn't an option for me. It's a must at my age and I have to do it the right way; working twice as hard due to my predisposition. I got a 3 week window with my brother to give him my answer. I'm contacting lawyers this morning to handle the documentation process. I wanted to get a packaged presentation together for you, but now I know specifically what you will be looking for. I can't see myself going back to prison. With this business, I can find a way to help build the communities I once tried to destroy. Some might say these are lofty dreams. I call it the outlook of a positive, forward thinking man."

"Wow Mr. Montenegro. I see you got yourself together. If your paperwork is in order, I won't stand in your way. You are one of the more fortunate ones with family behind you pushing you in the right direction. Come see me when you're ready Mr. Montenegro."

"Thanks. I appreciate that," Franchize said.

Ms. Johnson felt that this young man had an abundance of extremely positive potential that she rarely saw in her case load. Either that or he should have been an actor. She made up her mind to push his reporting back to once a month. If Mr. Montenegro could get his ducks in a row, she would make sure she got out of his way. The house check this morning gave her new hope for her son sitting on Rikers Island waiting to be released. She silently thanked Mr. Franklin Montenegro.

~ ~ ~

"Hey Billy! I know you were probably thinking I forgot to bring these back. Hope I'm not making you late," Franchize said.

"Son, that's the backup set in case I get a dose of Alzheimer's and lose the originals. I may be old, but I'm not crazy. Why don't you walk with me to work? It's only a little over four blocks."

"You know what, I got some time on my hands this morning so why not. Just excuse me for not being as sharp usual. I had a long night."

"No problem bub. But I want to be honest with you at the same time not complicating your life. I haven't been straight up with you," Billy lamented.

During a moment of silence following Billy's words, Franchize figured it would be best to keep his mouth shut until Billy got this off his chest. Whatever it is, it must be important. The look of torment on Billy's face contradicted the early summer signs of life. Franchize hoped Billy didn't have a problem with the use of the factory. Billy took a deep breath and began.

"It's my daughter. Angela has been hanging out with the wrong crowd. She has a 3.8 GPA, but decided to skip the semester for a break from all the pressures and bullshit she made up. But instead, she's partying and smoking weed. She is so smart and talented that it's breaking my heart to watch her grow up and at the last second, to take a turn for the worse. I don't know if it's a cry for attention or some sort of crisis that she is going through, but I have done everything I can do to try and nudge her back onto the right road. It's like she lost all faith in school and only wants to live on that computer. I have worked hard as I can to financially and emotionally make her being successful a possibility. Being stable and rock steady was a challenge I never thought I would be able to take on until her mother showed me the way through patience. My wife has hope of better days to come, but I see her glow diminishing as the days grow long. Did you know Jessica gave up a computer engineering career to raise Angela? She couldn't see someone else raising the life she brought into this world. Call it old school values passed down over generations. As the baby grew up, she taught her everything she knew about computers. She may not show it, but I know it's hurting Jessica to see what she taught daughter become her distraction. Maybe I just needed somebody to vent my frustrations. I don't know.

What I do know is that you got her by a couple of years but way less than what we have on her. I don't want to impose, but I'm backed into a corner and haven't truly tried everything unless..."

"Billy, say no more. Your struggle is my strife. I will be more than willing to do my best and try to talk some sense into her. You pick the place and time and I will be there. Just so you know, to avoid confrontation I'm going to pull her aside. It's the only way."

"Franchize, I wouldn't have it any other way. Tomorrow night we always have that good old fashioned Sunday dinner. It would be an honor. Do you eat pot roast?"

"And know it," Franchize said laughing. "But Billy, would you do me the honor of meeting my girlfriend Misha?

"Boy, you're going to bring to my eye. Of course me and the Mrs. got the space and food with more than enough interest to meet the fine lady that has caught your eye. 6:30 pm sound good?"

"Yea Billy, now I have to see how she is going to react. One way or the other, I will be there."

"One thing I learned about women with all these years I have on earth is that they will always go the people you call friends at least to try and get their measure. They are curious cats by nature."

"Spoken like a true preacher. Before I forget, do any lawyers that specialize in construction?"

"Yea, and they're local too. Jacobi and Canelo. Over on Steinway by the movie theater. They work hard and are affordable. Check them out."

"Good looking Billy. And don't go getting sentimental over pot roast tomorrow."

"I got you. I also got to let you know that the sentimental line you just shot is a Boomerang. Now give me a hug and get your way. You're making me late for work."

Franchize walked off with a new sense of direction and purpose. He would check out the lawyers then holla at his baby girl over at Creations.

CHAPTER 28

D etective Rodriguez was finishing up the day's paperwork when Agent Blanche approached his desk. Just seeing the man caused a buildup of irritation inside of him. The smug look on the Agent's face didn't help the situation either.

"Detective, it's good to see you. I look forward to hearing about the case you're building. How's it shaping up?"

"It's not shaping up in any form whatsoever. Your suspect appears clean. Hand sanitizer clean with nothing on the informant's channel or visually when we spot check with surveillance. I'm moving on and directing resources in another direction. Thanks for the tip but it didn't pan out this time around."

"Detective, surely you are capable. There is a lot riding on this case. I know you have a how shall we say this, vested interest in production. Rightfully so with that hard worked for promotion coming up. You wouldn't want to ruin that because you couldn't close a case now? Would you look into that again for me and give me the CI's file. I want to look over his accomplishments."

"We are done here Agent Blanche. Get the file from your department and get out of here. You're about as subtle as a walking skyscraper down 5th Avenue during rush hour. If you want something soft to squeeze, grab your nuts. Putting pressure over here is going to get you nowhere. Now if you will excuse me, I have a schedule to keep up."

Agent Blanche watched the detective walk away and knew that if he wanted anything done right, he had to do things himself. He wondered how these imbeciles operated and got anything done. Furry boiled beneath his skin. Franchize had to pay for his baby girl's life and it was time he evened the score.

By the time Detective Rodriguez made it home, he was behind schedule. His plans were quickly dissolving. The free flowers he got from Cecillia's had luxurious beauty radiating from them. Cecillia looked out from time to time for saving her son and scaring him onto the right path. Julio was also shaping up to be the best point guard in Queens this year. Julio might even be able to push the J.V. basketball team he coached for the local church into one of the top contenders for their division this coming season.

Once basketball started, nights like tonight would be limited, but it was worth the joy it brought the kids.

Cooking dinner was a breeze. While the candles he lit gave off the romantic ambiance he desired, he set the table and topped it off with some of the fresh flowers and bottle of wine. He could hear Victoria coming in and looked up.

"Honey, what's this? Is it my birthday already?" Victoria asked.

"No darling, it's a mini celebration."

"Okay, well let me freshen up first. Is it the promotion?"

"Nope. It's the fifth year since the first time I kissed you."

"Oh honey, you truly are the most touching man alive. Every day is a surprise with you. I have the perfect outfit. Want to watch me put it on?"

Lying in their bed cuddling, Victoria picked up tense vibes from her husband knowing after what they just did, he shouldn't still be awake. So she probed, "Honey, what's

On your mind?".

"Uh, it's nothing darling."

"Detective Gregory Rodriguez, something has your mind racing and I want to know what it is."

"Well, remember that FBI guy Blanche? He stopped by and threatened my pending promotion if I didn't dance to his tune. Let's go to the living room and I will play you all of the recordings and you tell me what you think."

After listening, Victoria erupted. "I will have his head on a platter and drink his blood! How dare this maggot talk to you like that! Oh wait until I talk to daddy in the morning. First will be his job. Second will be the case I'm presenting to my boss Monday morning. When I'm finished with this low life, he is going to wish he never met you. Nobody threatens my family and gets away with it. He won't contact you anymore. Wait and see."

Detective Rodriguez was stunned into silence. He had barely seen his wife angry so it was amazing and frightening to see her go ballistic. He was thankful she was on his side. She was acting like a war plane with its target in sight. Any minute now she was going to drop a bomb. He wanted to see how the Special Agent dodged it but first he wanted to find out how freaky his wife could become when infuriated.

CHAPTER 29

Misha had barked on Franchize for leaving without saying a word. It made her feel like a slut to wake next to an empty space. He should of stayed there after they made love. All he did was state facts about his situation and it made her second guess bugging out on him. Being hot and cold over Franchize drove Misha crazy. The level of trust he showed her by telling her his plans melted her heart. She knew she had to stop being so clingy because if she didn't, her chance at true love might disappear. Now she knew what he needed so she could try to help him. Her friend Brian from high school turned out to be a top notch accountant. After talking to him, he agreed to work Franchize's books at a discounted rate. Franchize was happy to hear that and keeping her man smiling became one of her focuses. She couldn't help feeling things would be good after all. Especially since Franchize hadn't stopped checking her out on the walk to Billy's.

When Billy opened the door, he surprised the hell out of her. He was an old white guy. She didn't know what was going on. Franchize had a white family as friends? Franchize truly seemed to be different everyday to her, but it was time to see what was up with this get up. She hoped Franchize wasn't selling these people drugs. If he was, she wouldn't be able to stop her foot from finding his neck.

After dinner Franchize took Billy's daughter Angela into the living room. She happened to be a quirky looking thing. Glasses, short black hair, and an infectious smile. She was full of energy and talked a thousand words a second trying to avoid the reason for Franchize talking to her on the side. She almost made him feel like he couldn't think fast enough to keep up with what she was saying, but he understood this to be her defense mechanism.

Angela knew she was in for it and at the end of her tirade was surprised by Franchize.

"Look Angela, blowing trees and not going back to school is only going to drag you into a downward spiral. You're a shooting star and smart. Yet you choose not to earn your way through life. If you're not going to school this semester, you're going to have to get a job.

"I need to bring my business into the internet world to boost what we got going on. I can't pay you much now, but how about $1,500 every two weeks and when things pick up, so does your pay and position?" Franchize thought that if she was set in her ways, the best thing he could do would be to put her under his wing.

"Franchize, let me get this straight. You're operating a business in the Stone Age with no net presence and you're going to pay me to bring it online? How about you give me a $500 advance tonight and in the morning you will have a website with my friends helping to build it? The money is for the junk food we need to kick off the hackathon we're going to have on your behalf. Trust me I got this. Just rundown everything I need to know about the business."

Franchize got lost in his conversation with Angela and an hour passed in the blink of an eye-breaking things down and answering well-thought questions. Hearing Misha laugh caught his attention and he knew it was time to join his lady.

~ ~ ~

Billy ended up taking the news of his daughter working for Franchize better than expected. Misha enjoyed herself and lined up dinner get-togethers for the future. Running around the last couple of days had exhausted Franchize, but excited him at the same time. Everything was moving at a fast pace now and he had to adjust. The lawyers charged him an arm and a leg, but they produced the documents that were needed out of thin air. Even Ms. Johnson was surprised at the packet Franchize put together. He felt good about the breathing room people gave him.

Business was already picking up. So much so that since he called his brother last Sunday night to thank him and to confirm he would take him up on his offer, Franchize hadn't slept much. With his past experience, he felt the best way to make more money would be to expand. After only a week, he already needed to bring his brother over to assist.

They met at the office Franchize recently leased. Within 24 hours of getting the keys, the place was completely renovated. New sheet rock was placed on the walls and debris was everywhere. Negro grabbed a milk crate and copped a squat while Franchize leaned on the new wall. Using the direct approach, Franchize locked eyes with his big brother and let him know the deal.

"Negro, things have picked up overnight and a steady increase in business is on deck for months. I called you in to let you take a look while I please my case for you coming over full time." Franchize started walking around as he continued. "If you know the preconceived notions the mind has, you can use them to your advantage in business."

Negro cut him off. "Franchize, I've seen the web site. How do you expect to make money with all the free work your advertising?"

"Negro, look at it like this, people would think our services cost less or that the 'free work' would be a giveaway if you display a wide range of "added services' for the same prices as the competitor. The key is to use what they fail to market to our advantage. The things we will be giving away for 'free' already come with the jobs. We're just broadcasting it now. This makes it look like the competitor is overcharging and like we're offering a deal."

"I still don't know if I can just over full time bro. You're really going to have to sell this to me with another example."

"Okay. You ever heard of the economist Amilcare Puviani?"

"Who's that? How do you even spell his name?"

"Negro, listen up. This economist called what we're trying to do the "fiscal illusion". Puviani said that people are more willing to pay taxes they cannot see. So rather than adding words like extra costs, we give customers a clearly visible price for the job. It's working and we need more workers to handle the demand.

Negro, we both know insufficient capital, web presence, and a company logo were obvious strikes against us. To combat that, I have brought some really talented people in. I got some money on hand to invest and I'm lining up a loan to further speed things up. What's the verdict?"

"My wife is going to kill me when she finds out, but you got me interested. I guess I can draft the most reliable and talented workers to fuel our expansion."

"Now that's the spirit big bro! It's time to take over the construction biz. Pure Quality Construction Co. on deck!"

CHAPTER 30

Victoria's father wasn't a man used to being denied many things. Privileged from birth, he went to the best schools. Every opportunity was afforded to him and he took advantage of them all. Money and influence were in abundance. His daughter, Victoria, is his only child. Congressman Patrick Montgomery called in some favors and they were at work. Some big wigs in the bureau had been briefed on the issue and the packet of documents with audio solidified their resolve. His wife moving within the aristocratic circles she was born into had also brought attention to the situation with Special Agent Blanche. Now they were scrambling over at FBI headquarters. Things take time, but after a full court press, they finally relented and put that maniac on leave pending departmental hearing. In 30 day, the ruling would come down and Congressman Patrick Montgomery was reassured of what the decision they were making.

The DA Mark Roman sat his ADA Victoria Montgomery -Rodriguez down and told her he passed the information on to a good friend of his. He knew the Federal Prosecutor for years and he told him the case was too weak for him to waste his time, but that he would hold onto it just in case. Mark wasn't going to tell Victoria that part. Finding out how strong and deep her family ties were had him worried. These were not people you angered. He also could sense that sooner than later this woman would be climbing the political ladder. He would keep his eye on her. It was imperative to stay in the good graces of friends like this. For now he had to play the politician and tell her that his friend would make Agent Blanche pay knowing otherwise.

Agent Blanche was furious. The walls were caving in on all sides and he had to do something about it. He lost the only family he had behind Franchize's actions. Now his career was in jeopardy. Word got around fast in the bureau and his days were numbered. It was time to quit playing around with this scumbag and do what needed to be done.

Driving through the streets of Queens, Blanche inspected all of the blocks around Franchize's apartment. Something would stand out to him. Blanche let all of his years of experience guide him. He flowed through traffic around the same blocks until the streets let up and traffic was almost non-existent. Pulling over to get some gas, the thought over what he observed. His sense of familiarity had evolved. Driving off, he pulled up on the far side of Franchize's building's parking lot and observed the scene. Feeling bold, he got out and walked into his building. Blanche pressed the button for the elevator and checked for cameras finding none. Checking the lobby and hallways with negative results, he made his way to the staircase. He saw the back door to the building as an older man exited it.

Blanche took the stairs to the second floor and got accustomed to the floor's layout. Knowing that this was all he needed to know what every floor looked like, he paid close attention. The heavy metal doors in the narrow hallways turned Blanche off. The middle section led to each separate hallway and to a staircase on the other side. Looking at the apartment numbers gave him idea of where Franchize's apartment would be on the fifth floor. Blanche left out the back door and stepped into what looked like a gated off sitting area with one way around the building. The short walk led him back into the parking lot and the front of the building. Satisfied with the knowledge he had gained, Blanche headed back to his car and went home.

Lying in bed, Blanche kept thinking about the heavy and slow front door. The slow elevator frustrated him and the heavy back door that only led back into the parking lot disgusted him. Then an idea hit him and a grin found its way onto his face. Things were going to pan out just right. It back to the drawing board.

Detective Rodriguez drove around making the usual rounds with his partner Detective Menelli when he spotted Agent Blanche getting into his car. Rodriguez tapped Menelli on the arm. "Hey, we got some action. Remember that agent I told you about? Well, there he goes."

Detective Menelli thought during Rodriquez' u-turn and said, "Looks like old boy was laying on his perp. Something's up cause unbilled overtime is something we don't do. Lay off him and give him some rope to hang himself. No point in tipping him off that we know he is up to no good."

Rodriguez lifted his foot off the gas pedal and slowed down. He didn't want to spook Agent Blanche with a tail. Menelli made a valid point. Turning down a side street, Rodriguez started to get the feeling that Blanche might have a personal beef with Franklin Montenegro. The wheels started to turn in his head and he asked his partner, "Have you heard from Gato lately?". Menelli looked at Rodriguez. "Well, I'll be damned. I thought he had been reporting to you over the last couple of weeks. You did say this Agent tried to get a hold of his file, right?"

Rodriguez was still thinking things over and simply said, "Yeah," while shaking his head. From the look on Menelli's face, he didn't like the coincidence either. It was time to shake down the neighborhood looking for Gato.

Driving down Astoria Boulevard, Rodriquez parked by where Gato last said he was working. Gato had informed him about a perp named Chino who was up and coming. The guy had a lot of clientele on a phone and two low level punks working for him on an attractive block. While they sat there parked, they reviewed what they knew about the agent and made links to Gato. It looked like the agent may have gotten to their Confidential Informant.

A heavy set young male took a known crack addict into a building. From his description, he fit the profile of one of Chino's pitchers. When he came out the building, they were in luck. Fat boy started to walk in their direction. As he got closer, Rodriguez and Menelli got out the car. Then, the unexpected happened. Just like that, for no reason they could fathom, fat boy took off running. Menelli screamed, "Police! Freeze!"

Menelli hated a runner and took off after him gaining on him with every stride he took. Rodriguez jumped in the car and planned to cut fat boy off. Menelli was well-built and the only reason he ran off duty was for situations like this. Fat boy jumped a waist high gate and started towards a project building. Menelli gained even more ground and fast. Fat boy's pants were sagging and it slowed him down. Menelli turned the gas up on his burners and started to lose balance before getting to the concrete. He wasn't going fat boys get away so he dove into the pitcher's back and crushed him into the side of the project building. Once the handcuffs were on, fat boy looked like a deer staring into headlights.

While Menelli was catching a breath, Rodriguez set to frisking the perp. At first, he turned up with nothing. He knew some of the tricks fake hustlers played so he ordered fat boy to kick his shoes off. Still Nothing. This time he can his fingers around his low strung pant line and got them hooked on a string attached to his pants button by the zipper. Up came a little velvet jewelry bag. Jackpot. 1. No jewelry in this bag. It was a bunch of bagged up crack rocks. Looking at his partner Rodriguez said, "Look at what we have here. Fat boy is going to be doing about 8 tubby tubbies upstate as someone's bitch."

Rodriguez gave Menelli the wink and the partners of 4 years were in their element. Menelli pushed the envelope. "Nope. He isn't going to do 8 years. Why are you being so optimistic? You see these scratches on my arm? Well I need a vacation so I'm throwing in assault on a police officer. We're going to need an ambulance cause I think he messed my back up when he kicked it. That would be an even 20 years on a plea bargain. You saw him hit me, right partner?"

Rodriquez enjoyed the fun so he didn't stop there. "Yea, I saw it partner. Oh shit, look at this. Fat boy even has some marked money. You should've brought some hamburgers with this tubby tubby because your charges are even more serious now. Your whole life is gone in one night. I hope you enjoyed it."

Christopher Ruiz was known as Gordo. He had never been in trouble with the law and couldn't see himself doing all that time in prison. His mother would go crazy if she found out what was happening right now. He always talked about how he hated snitches. A rat was something you didn't want as your label. But right now he was fighting for his life. Not caring about what people thought about him anymore, Gordo tried his hand. "Hey officer, maybe we could work out a deal. I got a whole bunch of info you need. I know everything that's going on out here. I just can't go to jail. I want to work for you. Just give me a chance to prove myself."

Detective Rodriguez pulled his partner to the side and said, "You do know this simple possession charge he is facing would have him out and running the streets again in less than a year tops. Might even get a program or drug court. I say we flip him at the precinct then run him through with a possessions charge. Get him released on his own recognizance and have him working for us within a couple of days. Some community service would do him good."

"I'm on board. Now we can find out what's up with our boy Gato. I hope the Lieutenant is in a good mood. Paperwork at this hour would make any man sour."

They took their new informant with them and played good cop bad cop the rest of the night. They pumped Gordo like a broke man being given an oil well.

CHAPTER 31

Franchize was on the move. Business was doing good so he didn't have time to do anything about the cocaine he had stashed. He had enough of the game and wanted to get rid of the drugs along with the .45 handgun. He called G Money up. From the conversations they had, Franchize was sure G Money would never leave the streets alone. All he could do was work on cleaning his act up. It was step by step process and it didn't feel right to get rid of the .38 he had in the stash. For now the coke and .45 would have to do.

Franchize met up with G Money in East N.Y. Driving the Camry gave him the safety of placing everything on the stash. He felt deep in his heart that G Money was a stand up brother, but they started to drift apart before he got locked up. At first they only had one phone. Not to confuse the customers they both answered the phone under the name Franchize. They were running through hoods.

G Money was the smooth type. Always attracting the ladies and getting them to do whatever he wanted. Franchize had limits to the things he would do in the name of a dollar. G Money though was a scandalous jump easy in the name of a penny. He did everything from opportunity pimping to lining brothers up to get robbed. Nowadays G Money strictly called shots. With a great connect and GMB under him, he enjoyed life in his freakish ways.

Franchize knew G Money better than anyone could. G Money was his friend in elementary school, JHS, and during the years of their "supposed" tenure in high school, which they never attended. G Money's mother was a crack whore. The men in her life beat G Money, kicking him out at all hours of the day and night. Some violated his mother and used her in front of him in ways that no son was supposed to witness their mother used just because they could.

There was never food in the fridge and she never bought him clothes. Times were hard for G Money. His mother was dark skinned, but he was brown skinned with curly hair and green eyes. He would never know who his father was, but by the time he was 8 years old, he had it figured out. Somebody had used his mother the way they sometimes do in front of him and left to never come back. G Money hated that he had to stay. It made him bitter inside. It also made him wiser beyond his years and gave him the twisted outlook he had towards women that was set in stone. He hated them. There were only two women he had any semblance of respect towards- Franchize's Mother and sister.

Whenever G Money was hungry, he had access to a full fridge. Every night he ate dinner before going home. When he got kicked out, which was a lot, he could buzz the bell and Mom would let him in. G Money slept on the couch and some nights he told Franchize's mother things that made her cry while she held G Money in her arms. She never looked at him differently and treated him like one of her own. By junior high school, he was calling her Titi Mia, *My Aunt*.

They shared clothes and mom didn't hesitate to bark at G Money when he messed up just like she did the rest of her kids. When they started to commit crimes, she knew she couldn't do anything about it. She met G Money's mother a couple of times and knew that was a dead end for help. So she looked for diversions. Nothing worked. They were on autopilot heading towards destruction. All she could do was stand aside and watch her boys turn into monsters.

Franchize grew violent towards people who weren't related to him and ended up moving out with G Money at an early age. G Money was just as violent, but with a sick twist. He even liked to break people's bones in ways that would make them handicapped in area for life. Franchize never tried to do it, but if it happened, he didn't lose any sleep over it. When Franchize cut someone, one or two slashes would do. When G Money went to work, he made sure the guy's face looked like shredded paper. He wouldn't stop until something horrible happened to the poor soul that crossed his path.

What jump started their fallout was when G Money began offering girls blunts laced with crack in order to flood a new hood. He enjoyed getting them hooked and jumped on the opportunities to pimp them. He shared the money with Franchize, but he began feeling dirty holding that money.

Just as they put the Get Money Boys together, he got locked up for killing his worker E Banger. The bozo tried to push his work on Franchize's phone. G Money pulled his coat to what was happening and when they ran down on son, things got out of control. E Banger talked like a tough guy and Franchize used his tough guy neutralizer without thinking. He let off four shots into E Barger's chest with a 9 mm. G Money grabbed the phone. It was the money motivator and was needed like a breath of fresh air.

Franchize was identified by a neighborhood watchman and a crack head. They wanted to know who was with him, but he kept his mouth shut. After two years of going to court, they offered him 12 years flat or pick 12 jurors. Franchize didn't feel lucky and knew 12 was better than 25 to life. With that life on the back, you could be spinning the yard forever. People that have been up top know that this isn't the suburbs where you walk on the yard. In prison, you're walking into a secured, locked off, gun towering yard. There aren't too many directions to go when spinning unless you're playing ball or working out. When you stop for a rest, drink or seat, you're not just chilling, you're posting up. Always on point. Watching the CO's watch you and paying attention to those rats looking for an extra tray of slop or whatever they get to tell on you.

Franchize was good his whole bid. G Money sent money and whatever Franchize needed. G Money even sent him ladies from time to time so he could have fun. That's how he met that crazy broad Stacey. Real nigga shit. G Money knew Franchize kept it real when he didn't drag him along for the body. It never crossed Franchize's mind to snitch on G Money. Franchize knew the system was twisted. People who rat know they got protection. Other people knowing who the rats are leave them alone. They have an aura around them that says if you touch them, they are telling on you. The goal is to get out of prison. So the old school ways of snitched get stitches is dying slowly but surely. You got your convicts, inmates, and offenders.

After Franchize's first day inside he knew he was a convict. Prison made him wiser. It gave him the ability to think things through. There was once a time that Franchize didn't realize he could see things clearer if he went through every detail with his eyes open as if he had all the time in the world. Analyzing G Money took a lot of thought. It's why he tried to limit his meetings with him, Sure enough, Franchize ended up figuring out more than he wanted about G Money. For now, he had to keep those thoughts suppressed. G was good at reading body language. Therefore, tipping his hat and showing G Money his thoughts wasn't a good idea.

When Franchize pulled up on G Money's block in East N.Y, you could feel the tension in the air. You couldn't just step on the wrong block with any type of bling. The wolves' eyes would light up and their pockets caching. Franchize spent a lot of time around different brothers from all over the state and boroughs. He felt he could draw a few lines and a lot of the people would fit within them. It was all about knowing the lay of the land and meeting enough of the same personalities to begin a sketch.

G Money was looking for new ways for people to fall victim to his sadistic enjoyment. Franchize noticed his clothes looked weird. Tight suit pants, fitted red and black lumberjack button down and combat boots. Eccentric wasn't the word. His face was straight gangsta trying to hide behind aviator glasses, but even his forced smiles looked out of place. People who knew G Money kept out of his way and enough word was spread so the stick kids that valued life more than money stayed away.

Franchize made himself obvious by rolling to a stop in front of where G was posted. G and a couple of rough leaking dudes eyed Franchize's whip with murder on their mind. Franchize rolled down the window. A look of recognition flashed across G Money's face and he said something to the people with him. The gunners looked away and G made his way to the passenger side,

Jumping in G Money greeted him. "Bro, what's the good? Holla and express the move". Franchize couldn't do anything but smile. "We what's good. Plotting with our vision is the view. Franchize fell right in line like no more than 24 hours passed since he last ran with GMB. It felt good and he knew it was a dangerous feeling. The feeling of nostalgia was so strong that he almost resented the change.

"Speak easy." G Money said,

"Minus 3. Fruits of labor," Franchize said.

"Revive a historic figure."

"Escobar's alive."

"How old"

"600."

"Liquidators?"

"Yea. Bonus treat. Second skin."

"Back or front? Street number?"

"Only move front blocks. 45th street,"

"I got 18 for you, plus 2 regifts. We good?'

"We always good."

"Make a left on Pennsylvania and keep going till I tell you to pull over and park."

Franchize started to relax after negotiations were over. He knew he could get more money if he broke the work down and set up shop. He could probably even get more money selling it that someone else. Prices must have gone through the roof for G Money to part with 30 a gram at a discount. Franchize heard about a drought, but prices must be more volatile than the stock markets during a close presidential race. The regifts had Franchize intrigued. He wondered what they were.

They walked up to a brownstone building. G Money had the whole second floor to himself. The kitchen was a mess, but the living room was clean. Franchize was confused at the differences between the rooms, but he paid it no attention and sat down on the leather couch. Looking around he noticed there wasn't a T.V. It didn't say much about G Money, but Franchize didn't know how long he was going to be getting the money together. To entertain himself, he placed everything on the coffee table and took apart the .45.

Franchize had lost his train of thought when G come back from a room off to his right. He had a tray with the money, a scale, and box on it. After setting the tray down, G Money picked the coke and examined it. This wasn't the movies and a person like

G Money armed with cocaine experience could tell it's good by its smell and look. G Money weighed it then passed Franchize the money. Franchize flipped through it and saw it was all crispy hundred dollar bills. He wasn't going to sit there and count out 18 thousand. He piled it on the scale in two rows and it read 180 grams. Franchize understood that any dollar denomination from a single to a hundred dollar bill all weighed a gram. He felt like G was testing him to see if he would pull an armature move.

Without saying another word G Money passed Franchize the box. In it was an exotic watch that Franchize knew must have been extremely expensive. He couldn't help himself and he put it on. It fit perfectly. Even its weight was comforting. A voice in Franchize's head screamed it was too good to be true, but beauty and elegance of the watch drowned out all sound of reason. Franchize thanked G and the grin on his face was trying to tell him something. Unfortunately, Franchize couldn't get a read on it. While he started to read into the possibilities of that well known grin, G pulled out a set of keys. Franchize was just at the cusp of grasping the memory that linked the grin when he was distracted and he let it drown in the depths of his mind.

"It's a Ford F-150, 2 years old but for my brother the CEO, this should be a valued asset. Sis told me how good you were doing so I'm regifting you something I can't use, but that you need. I already checked uncle Tito for a stash so you already know." Franchize was at a loss for words. He needed more trucks. Not wanting to deny himself the pleasure he was feeling, he took the gifts and gave G Money a hug.

When Franchize walked out, G looked at his back with disgust. He felt Franchize was slipping and he was now soft and weak. There was no half-stepping and Franchize should of known that. G Money was mad that Franchize wanted to pay Uncle Sam for doing business. He felt homicidal towards Franchize for turning his back on him and GMB. G thought prison weakened his mind and made his boy lose his edge. The old Franchize would of seen through things. It was a shame he failed the test. One that may cost Franchize dearly. He should have turned down that $20,000 watch. G wondered how Franchize could not see. He fooled everyone but G Money. G would expose Franchize as a humpty dumpty ass nigga. He felt he was the wind that blows. No matter which side of the fence Franchize fell on, he would break him for turning his back on him and GMB. G Money continued to seethe and let his hatred seep into the cup of tea he was going to make Franchize drink. Putting into motion his chess pieces on the board he created, G Money fell back to watch the action

CHAPTER 32

Detective Rodriguez got good information from fat boy, but it also troubled him.

It looked like Gato and Chino up and disappeared. The steady stream of busts and surveillance operations kept him busy. Yet, not only one, but two people vanishing kept nagging at him. Remembering Gato kept a GPS device on him to verify his location during testimony, an idea hit Rodriguez like divine intervention. Opening up his laptop, he set to running the desired program. Clicking through the settings, frustration started to kick in. Gato's last known location was a parking lot. That didn't help Rodriguez much. His digging hit pay dirt! It looked like Cato went to a factory then to the parking lot where his signal died.

Still stuck, Rodriquez ran a different program on the department's computer. He put in the parking lot's coordinates from his lab top. At once, his interest was sparked. On the same date and around the same time, a car exploded and was found on fire. Now that he had something to work with, he went over the evidence collected. After going through every detail several of times, Rodriguez came away disappointed. More questions were popping up than answers. How could Gato's belt be in a burning car, but no body was found? Wanting to make sure and rule out certain possibilities, Rodriguez went to the crime lab's specialist on fires.

"Hey Rhonda, do you remember that blow up recently in a parking lot by Con Ed?" Rodriguez asked.

"Read the file and don't waste my time. You know better than that, " Rhonda said.

"Okay okay, don't shoot. I saw your name in the file and wanted to ask if it's possible human remains burned up in the fire?"

"Do you take me for a fool? There were no human remains and if there were, it would have been hard to miss the bones. The reason being…"

"It's okay Rhonda. I just needed to double check. Sorry to bother you. I owe you one."

Detective Rodriguez was on a new trail. If Gato didn't go with his GPS from the factory, it meant he stayed and his belt left, Gato could have left in another direction but the combination of his disappearance around the same time as Chino gnawed at him. Gato was pumping Chino for information and helping to build a case against him. Anything could have happened and he hoped one didn't kill the other and get low. Rodriguez broke his suspicions down to his partner and off they went.

The factory didn't turn anything up except that it was by the river. Harbor Patrol gave a negative to bodies in the water. Rodriguez knew it didn't take much to sink one in the East River. The plant The plant manager Billy didn't see anything out of place when he opened up. The only possible break when he bumped into Joe from the Abscondering unit. He looked for a parolee that failed to report around the same time Gato and Chino went missing. The violator's street name was Scrappy. Things were getting complicated so he tagged Scrappy's file. When they rounded him up, Rodriguez wanted a chance to question him. For now he would have to be content pumping fat boy for a lead or two to find the missing informant.

~ ~ ~

Pay Day started to get trickles of information about a Spanish dude named Franchize that came home from up top recently rocking his watch. Payday wanted to kill the fool dumb enough to run up into his baby mother's crib and yap him for 2 million and some jewelry. He wished was there when it happened. Him and his shooters would of made Swiss cheese out of whoever acted like they wanted problems. He felt secure nobody could get at him. His stashes were vulnerable when he wasn't around.

Pay Day traveled in a bulletproof Range Rover with the gunners following at a distance. The dope spots the owned generated him millions every month. The more money he got, the more paranoid he became. Pay Day was too high up the chain of command to even be around the blocks anymore. What called him back was when a fool hits one of his stash cribs. "*They always end up dead,*" thought Payday. Messages like that had to be sent because if not, the wolves would think he was sweet meat. He heard whispers about a Brooklyn cat, but this Queens fool rocking his watch sealed the deal. Payday wondered what went through the minds of fools crazy enough to think they could home from prison and rob anyone without consequences. His BX street team was dangerous. Not to mention all of the hungry gangstas. Pay Day put 100 thousand on Franchize's head knowing it was a full plate of food for the wolves. The old man Ponce put one of his best to track Franchize down. A Puerto Rican fresh from the Island named Cuco. Their record with Payday was great and this was the biggest contract he had given them. He wanted to make sure Franchize got touched the right way. For now he went to work finding out how this Q- Boro foolio found out about his stash.

He knew Melissa wasn't dumb enough to play herself. His shorty would take a charge for him and keep her mouth shut. The type of loyalty she gave him he couldn't buy. He knew people paid attention to his every move and could put one and one together to find out who his ladies were, but this hit a little too close to home. His gut told him to take a closer look at Brooklyn, but he had the same feeling last time when a Washington Heights lemon got caught slipping rocking one of his chains. Sooner or later things would fall into place. With that amount of money on Franchize's head, someone would be coming to collect soon. Who didn't look forward to a payday?

CHAPTER 33

Agent Blanche took a swing from the bottle of Southern Comfort. He was drunk and sweating. The AC didn't help and looking through the windshield, he could tell it was a cool evening. Boiling with rage kept him alert. His Oxford shirt clung to his chest while he gripped his government issued Glock. Taking a gulp, he felt the liquid ignite as it made its way down his throat. A few heart beats later, it spread a cold warmth across his chest. That hollow cavity that grew over the years where his heart belonged was now vast like the tundra. No matter how hot the drink got him, his true self was a polarized frost bite.

Franklin Montenegro walked out of his building and his heart rate increased. Blinded by hate, he took one last swing and dropped the bottle to his lap as he forcefully opened the car door. Stumbling into the parking lot, the bottle of Southern Comfort went skating across the asphalt. All he could do was smile at how something as fragile as glass didn't break as it skidded to a stop.

Walking towards Franchize, the 9 mm Glock trembled in his hands. The object of his hatred stood illuminated by the lone yellow light above the building's entrance. Every step took him closer to the sphere of brightness from the shadows. Blanche couldn't wait any longer.

Leveling his gun, he let off one shot. Seeing the scum spin around and dive for the building door, he let off two more shots. He noticed à woman that Franchize was dragging into the hallway and it gave him pause for a second. His heart pounded and sweat got into his eyes. Looking at the bloody mess in front of him, he locked eyes with Franchize. The scum was knelt on the floor before a bleeding woman. Raising the gun in shaky hand, he put Franchize's wide chest in direct line with the barrel of his instrument of destruction.

"Before I kill you, I want to know why you would trick an innocent young girl into smoking crack?!" Franchize looked down at his bloody hands. The pool of Misha's life source grew and he could almost feel her asking him why as she slipped in and out of consciousness. Making eye contact with his grim reaper, Franchize began to understand death's question. His life rewound before his eyes. The anger he felt when he found out what G Money was doing back then came into focus and jumped into slow motion. Becoming at peace with himself, Franchize began to talk. "Go ahead and kill me! The man that gave your daughter that sickness will live!"

All Franchize could do was laugh at the thought that something he wasn't willing to do came back to haunt him. Agent Blanche was confused. He knew this scum before him would say anything to live, but why those words. He hesitated to pull the trigger. He heard the yell "freeze" loud and clear. The word itself erupted like a thunderbolt of sound that stunned him so much he instinctively turned in its direction only to be struck by lightning. Before he was able to comprehend what had happened, the cold hollow in his chest overflowed with a warmth that brought comfort.

Detective Rodriguez and his partner were sitting side by side laying on Franchize's building. Fat boy produced a gem when he broke down the fight Franchize had with Chino in front of his girlfriend's salon, Creations. Rodriguez was mentally going over the questions he was going to toss at Franchize when he saw him step out of his building. He didn't have a warrant, but tying up loose ends never hurt. Montenegro's parole was a card he could use to question him.

As he and his partner got out of the unmarked crown vic, a shot rang out. Two more came right behind it. "Call it in!" Rodriguez said to his partner. Pulling his gun out of his holster he could see the shooter now entering the building. With his partner on his heels, they reached the entrance in no time. Observing the situation at a glance gave him no other option but to enter the building with his gun trained on the perp. Montenegro was kneeling over a woman with blood everywhere and a gun was pointed at his chest. Screaming "Freeze!" caused the perp turned towards his direction gun in hand.

He squeezed off the first shot and his partner followed suit. They riddled the man with bullet after bullet until he went down. Just as fast as the shooting started, it ended. With a look at his partner, Rodriguez assessed they weren't hurt. He automatically went over and kicked the gun away for the perp he now recognized as Agent Blanche. Looking at the scene in front of him brought up a rage he had hidden deep down inside. Seeing Agent Blanche's rapidly spreading pool of blood touch the edge of the woman's own made him look at Franchize with new eyes. He watched Franchize stay on his knees holding the woman, oblivious to what was happening around him. Rodriguez heard the ambulance in the back ground and a trickle of uniformed officers started to arrive, but Franchize stayed in place. With his rage in check, Rodriguez couldn't help but notice the malevolent chaos simmering behind Montenegro's eyes. It made his own concerns seem petty, almost nonexistent. Such raw emotion made the air around him seem to hum. It gave Rodriguez the notion that extreme undercurrents would make Franchize explode at any second like a volcano.

When the ambulance arrived, Franchize moved for the first time since he arrived on the scene. Franchize got out of their way and let them get to work on the young woman. His movements were rational and that surprised Rodriguez. It made him wonder. There had to be something more to Franklin Montenegro. The files he read could only tell him so much. He knew better than to treat them like the Gospel because that would put him at a disadvantage. A closed minded bias point of view would get him nowhere.

"Mr. Montenegro, I am Detective Rodriguez. Come with me and I will make sure you get a ride to the hospital. I'm guessing you want to be there for the young woman. But first you need to answer some questions."

"You want answers to questions? Well, so do I. You know my name and I haven't said it yet. I got no answers cause I don't know shit. I need to be in the hospital waiting for any type of information and I can't go. My curfew kicks into place in less than 10 minutes." Franchize said the last sentence with such contempt that it almost made Rodriguez second guess the parole officer who made that rule up.

Rodriguez was running out of time. Soon he would be relieved for discharging his fire arm. "That guy getting worked on, he is a Federal Agent." The look of confusion on Franchize's face was genuine and did nothing but bring in another truckload of questions. Out the corner of his eye he saw his escort and the detectives that were going to be taking over the investigation. "Before I go, do you know Gato and Chino?"

"I got important phone calls to make to family members. I don't have time for your game of 21 questions."

"Well, you will for me. I am Detective Carter and I have to ask you about what happened tonight."

The questioning from Detective Carter felt more like an interrogation. Once he got the chance, he called his sister and Evelyn to ask them if they could make it to the hospital in his place. Franchize thought about the police contact and knew it was enough to get him a one year violation if parole wished to pursue the issue. Not risking a curfew violation made him feel guilty. Having bullets meant a strike for him. Misha destroyed the foundation he was trying to build upon. Taking responsibility was one thing Franchize never shied away from and the waves of guilt that washed over him only frustrated him even more.

A little voice in his head echoed over and over that he was coward for not giving a fuck about parole and going to the hospital after curfew. His lady needed him right now and he stood hiding in his room. Then reason kicked in again. He could give her more over the course of a year outside than he could over the course of a couple hours when he wouldn't even be able to see her. He still felt dirty over the choice he made so he jumped in the shower.

Tossing and turning all night, Franchize only got to sleep in bits and pieces. The latest update was that Misha was stabilized and would be able to receive visitors shortly. Waiting on the clock to let him out in the morning had been agonizing. It felt as if life played a cruel joke on him. In prison, he felt as if time didn't move fast enough. Especial when he neared his last days. The feeling of déjà vu caught him off guard. Being free was a joke when his crib became a prison.

On his way to the hospital, Franchize felt reassured he made the right decision because his gut was nagging him. He had a feeling he was being watched and followed. Riding in the left lane, he steadily looked into the pick-up truck's mirrors to spot the blue minivan which kept popping up. Switch lanes to catch his exit, he spotted the same van on the off ramp. His senses sharpened as he became on point. In Franchize's lifetime, he knew that if no precautions were taken when dealing with coincidences, things could get ugly fast. Thinking it was the police playing "watch the parolee", he made sure all his paperwork for the truck was in order as he got out and headed into the hospital.

Alexis and Evelyn greeted him with bloodshot eyes. They looked as if they hadn't slept in days. They already had the green light to go in, but for the past half hour Alexis and Evelyn waited for him. Making his way through the lobby he spotted a Mexican woman selling flowers and he bought a dozen as they jumped in the elevator.

Franchize was the first one to go in the room and before the rest of the troops could follow they heard Misha's painful of "get out!". Stunned and frozen in place, Alexis and Evelyn waited outside. They heard another cry, but this time the words were "I hate you!".

The silence after that unnerved them. Then Franchize spoke and they strained to hear his words. "Misha, I love you. You make me right on every wrong day and glow on every dark night. I know I should be the one where you are right now and it's killing inside. Baby…"

Misha cut him off with enough ice in her voice to give the ladies standing outside enough foresight to stay put where it was warm.

"I never want to see you again. Get out of my life. Leave now! You're a gangsta and your lifestyle isn't going to destroy my life. I knew better from the start and I let you con me into laying in this bed with bullets meant for you. I refuse to live a lie. I hate you!"

They stood out as they watched Franchize exit the room. The flowers he had were gone and the look on his face screamed murder. Alexis went to follow her brother, but Evelyn caught her arm. "Let him go. Sometimes a man needs a moment to himself."

Driving back to his neighborhood, he didn't notice the minivan following him. Misha's words bounced around his mind like a .22 caliber bullet killing him. Her last sentence hurt more than anything. Just when he found a woman that made his heart beat to a tune he could enjoy forever, she changed the station. He wondered how he could change her mind and decided the best he could do was give her time. If it was meant to be, it would. Wanting to distract himself, he pulled over at his office on Northern Boulevard and got lost in his paperwork.

By the time he finished up, it was dark outside. He had worked through lunch and dinner. Hunger drove his movements now. Enjoying the cool night air, he made his way to the truck. That's when he noticed the minivan across the street start driving in his direction. At first he thought it was black until it passed under a street light. The color made the hairs on the back of his neck stand up. Staying on the sidewalk while the van came down the other side of the two-way street gave him a sense of safety.

He passed the parked cars on his way to the truck. The van came to a stop directly across from him and the side door flew open. A masked AK-47 wielding gunman jumped out and let off a burst of shots his way. Franchize took off running. That first spray of bullets hit the wall and he could feel his face stinging from brick chips as he zigzagged down the block. Looking over his shoulder, Franchize's executioner came into view as he stepped onto the same sidewalk. Before he even heard the shots ring out, he dove onto the hood of a parked car. More shots rang out. A long burst of deadly bullets tore up the side of the car he dove onto. His chest hit the hood at an awkward angle with his shoulder hitting the floor first. Using momentum to continue the roll, he was back on his feet in no time running for his life.

Still looking over his shoulder, Franchize didn't see the man ducking low by the side of the car in the street. The lower half of his body hit her at a high speed sending him flying through the air and skidding across the asphalt that ripped the skin on his forearms. Panicking, Franchize started to squeeze his way under the nearest car as more shots rang out. This time the echo of shot after shot was longer. The asphalt jumped at the contact from the bullets and bit into his arm. The thud of projectiles slamming into the ground so close to him stopped his breathing. He thought he was dying. Then just as fast as things started, they ended. He could barely hear the van peeling off. The blood pumping through his ears kept up a drum beat staccato that rivaled the West Indian Day Parade. After a couple of seconds, Franchize started to get his breathing under control. Sliding out from underneath the car and standing up, he felt himself and instantly knew he wasn't shot. He looked up into the night sky and for the first time in a long time Franchize said a prayer.

Hearing the sirens in the background brought him back to reality. Rushing to the corner, he cut down the block. Pulling out his celly, Franchize called a cab to meet him three blocks down. By the time he got there, the cab was pulling up. A cop car came slowly down the block. Acting as normal as he could, Franchize jumped in giving the driver directions. The cabbie wouldn't stop looking at his face in the rear view mirror and checking out the cops strolling by. With a thick Spanish accent the cabbie asked, "Hombre, wha happen to you face?"

"My girl caught me in her house with another girl. She took the keys to the car she bought me. So I left the other girl behind to save the rest of my face from her hands."

"Haha. You crazy hombre. I like you."

The cab driver kept on laughing and drove past the cop car. Franchize slumped into his seat and thought of his next move. Getting close to his house, Franchize remembered a conversation between

Misha and Evelyn. Evelyn had completed a medical assistant class, but she earned more money doing hair. He wanted to get cleaned up and stay away from a hospital at the same time.

"Hey, pull over right here. Take this $50 and keep the change."

Papi lit up like a Christmas tree. At least somebody was having a good day he thought.

Franchize knocked on Evelyn's door and stood waiting for a couple minutes. He began to believe she wasn't home. Not wanting to be exposed for a long period of time he was ready to walk off. Two steps away, he heard the door open and turned to find Evelyn in a robe with a towel wrapped around her head. Now he understood the delay. Evelyn looked at Franchize's face and pulled him inside without hesitation.

"What happened to you?" Evelyn asked. "I need somebody to clean me up. No hospitals, no questions. Can you do it?"

Evelyn looked uncertain checking his wounds out. "I think I can. It's just a bunch of scrapes and abrasions."

"You got what you need?"

Grateful she stole a couple emergency kits from school she said, "Yea, wait right here."

Wanting to get close to a gun, Franchize changed plans. "Hey Eve, get dressed. We're going to my place. You got an extra t-shirt big enough for me?"

"Yea but it's old"

"Good enough. Ima be in the bathroom."

CHAPTER 34

"Cuco, what do you mean you mean you think you got him? I do not pay you to think! Did you get him, yes or no?"

"Old man, wha you want me to say? I shoot the AK. He took off like rabbit. Jumping, dodging, turning. Wish you see this guy. Shooting at rabbit once second and a frog the next. When I go to get him the last time, he turned into a snake and slither you know. Under a car he go! Hahaha Fucking guy. If he no dead, I get him next time. I used one clip. Next try, I use two. He no get away you see."

"Muchacho, this is not a game! Stupid people play around. Those are the ones that die! Coco you don't see, it's over. Rules are rules. We moving on."

"Old man, I getting tired of million rules with no million dollars. This money Pay Day has is two to five jobs in one. $100,000 dollars then you take your slimy fingers and get a greasy 40 percent. I think you're a piece of shit that steals from me. You so pussy you no even pull trigger no more huh? Well I got a gift for you. Early retirement."

Cuco pulled out a .380 and let the whole clip go into the old man. He turned on JR, the old man's secretary. "You work for me now. You run, you lie, you steal, you die. Comprende?"

JR seeing no other option available to live said "Yes boss, I will even get in touch with Pay Day to let him know when the job is done, you will personally pick up the money. I handle everything else boss. Okay?"

"Get this piece of shit out of here. This basement is my new office. I want it clean when I come back JR. Don't let me down chamaquito."

Cuco left on a mission. First he needed some sleep and a new car. Then this rabbit, frog, snake man was going to die.

~   ~   ~

Detective Rodriguez walked into Misha's room. Looking at the young woman bundled up with a cast on her forearm gave him pause. She truly was a lucky young woman. A bullet to the right shoulder, right forearm, and right side of the abdominal all went through and through. Rodriguez hoped she was strong enough to answer some questions that bothered him.

"Ms. Davis, I'm Detective Rodriguez and have a few questions if you don't mind."

Misha looked at him with contempt etched on her features and said "If you're going to ask me the same set of dumbass questions, you might as well get out now and read one of the other cops notes."

"No, Ms. Davis, the questions are about a Mr. Franklin Montenegro."

Her fears were confirmed by the detective's interest in Franchize. Wanting to know what he was getting at, Misha nodded her head.

"Do you know people by the names of Gato and Chino?"

The clear confusion on Misha's face made Rodriguez press the issue. "Chino was the kid Mr. Montenegro had an altercation with in front of Creations."

"Detective, let's not play games. Don't waste my time by asking me questions you already know the answer to and all that. What is it you want to know?"

"Has Mr. Montenegro ever talked to you about hurting anyone?"

"No."

"Has he to your knowledge come across any of those two individuals after the Creations incident?"

"No."

"Do you know where Mr. Montenegro was on August 14th? I am not talking about daytime. Specifically between 1 and 7 am."

Misha thought for a second. She was about to say no, but that date kicked off memories of the first time they made love.

Detective Rodriguez spotted the hesitation on her face and prompted, "Ms. Davis?"

"Well, I think I do. We were together that night, but I fell asleep and when I woke up at 6 am, he was already gone. I know it had to be after 1 am when I fell out. I just don't know how much after."

"Well, did he have a phone that night? If he did, do you have the number?"

"I got the number. I just want to know what this is all about. Tell me something useful and I will give it to you."

"I got some useful info for you. The man that shot you is a federal agent that went rogue. He was so drunk, his aim was off. If not, I'm sure he wouldn't have missed. The agent is still alive in critical condition. And by the way, that number could prove Mr. Montenegro wasn't involved in the disappearance of Gato and Chino."

Misha more confused now than ever struggled with the information she received. She thought she was shot over some stupid street beef. She needed time to process everything because her feelings towards Franchize started to conflict.

"Detective, if what you find out is good or bad would you tell me?"

Not want to pass up a good lead and at the same time cross off a suspect on the disappearance of his confidential informant, he agreed.

~ ~ ~

Franchize woke up to the soft curves of a woman under his sheets. The last thing he remember before passing out was lying on his bed fully clothed. Now he was in his boxers with Evelyn wearing panties and the t-shirt she let him borrow. His dick was hard like a piece of wood. Grabbing his morning stiffy to put it in a more comfortable position brought Evelyn to turn over to face him.

Before he could say anything, she shut him up by grabbing his extension. Without thinking Franchize lifted her shirt. He brushed his lips over and sucked on her Hershey kisses. Pulling her hair back, he placed his lips to her exposed neck. Evelyn surprised by pushing him on to his back. She tossed the bed sheet to the side and pulled off his boxers. Taking him in both hands, she began to suck and slurp, devouring him in a mad frenzy. Pulling out of Evelyn's wet and warm mouth was almost enough to drive him insane. She crawled seductively to the center of the bed and arched her back like a cat.

Franchize got up and walked to where her ass faced him and enjoyed the view. Grabbing her by her ankles, he pulled her almost all the way, off the bed. When he let go of her legs, he could hear her feet land on the floor. She jiggled her ass, bouncing on her tip toes while her body laid flat on the bed. Her thick fat ass enticed him as wave after wave rolled over her flesh with every bounce.

Lust controlled his movements like it was the puppeteer. He grabbed her panties with both hands and ripped them in half, exposing her crotch. Sticking two fingers inside her sweet spot found nothing but a pool of juicy juices. As his fingers slid out, his joy stick began its penetration. With both hands on her hips, he grudge fucked her. He pounded her pussy with no remorse. Every ounce of anger that built up since his release from prison was placed behind every powerful stroke. Hearing her moan with pleasure drove Franchize to give everything he had with each pump. Evelyn found his rhythm and tried her best to throw her pussy back in tune with Franchize's assault. His roughness and size made her cum back to back. She could feel her juices running down the inside of her thighs all the way to her ankles. She fell in love with the pain and pleasure losing control brought her.

Franchize realized too late that his little soldiers were ready to spill forward. He just couldn't stop himself. Thrust after thrust his soldiers shot from him. When the last of his troops left the ship he had parked in deep waters, he stayed there, parked for several moments. With his heart still racing, Franchize knew he fucked up big time.

They were getting cleaned up in the bathroom when Evelyn asked, "Papi, you want breakfast?"

Not wanting to play games and get Evelyn attached to him, he lead her to the futon in the living room and sat her down.

"Eve, what I gots to say is more important than breakfast."

Looking up at Franchize with curiosity on her face she smiled and said "Franchize, I don't kiss and tell. I'm a grown woman and what happened, happened. You won't hear a word of this from me. Now if you let me make you something to eat; I can get on my way to picking Misha up. I have a busy day ahead of me so will an egg and cheese sandwich do?"

Surprised by Evelyn's words he weighed the possibilities of what could happen. Fucking up didn't seem too bad when she put it like that. If Evelyn wouldn't blow it up he sure as hell wouldn't tell on himself. "I want my sandwich with ketchup and my coffee black."

CHAPTER 35

C uco got his hands on an old black Honda Accord. He parked up a half block away from Franchize's place with the front of the building in sight. He began to relax, enjoying the goodies he bought to last him the rest of the afternoon. Finding out his rabbit escaped from his trap gave Coco a new found respect for his future victim. This time he would make it his duty to get up close and personal. Now the only jumping around would be Franchize's soul when it leaps from his body after his .357 splits his head wide open.

Day dreaming about the money and all the ways he could kill Franchize distracted him. Focusing only on the building out the driver side window allowed a crackhead to creep around from the passenger side. He sprayed water on his windows and tried to clean them with a twisted squeegee. Getting tight, Cuco put the big bag of Doritos on his lap where the .357 sat and lowered the passenger side window.

"Oye! You stinky motherfucka, wha fuck you do? Fucking crackhead, don't touch my shit. You lucky I don't crack yo ass! Fuck out of here."

"Okay okay. I don't want no problems. You got it," Flaco said.

Mad his lay low spot was hot, Cuco threw the car in gear, and drove off. Flaco felt there was something suspicious with that dude and went to chill in front of Franchize's building. He hoped his boy would look out for him for putting him on to the stick up the kid was plotting. People thought him to be paranoid or high when he brought things like this to their attention. He wanted, no, needed Franchize to believe in him. Life seemed easier when he was smoking crack. Checking himself into rehab a couple weeks ago helped him get clean. Finding out they really couldn't help him past giving advice put him back on the juice. He understood now that he wanted to quit because he was tired of using. It disgusted him enough to have the strength to put crack down. Not having a ounce of self respect and dignity the day Franchize came home was the last straw. Franchize gave him a hug and money when everyone else wanted to humiliate him and prey on his addiction to take in order to take every dollar he had.

Being sober made him to realize how weak he had become. The drive to get enough money for a room and some clothes kept him from falling back into the mess of a crackhead's life. Even though he knew he still looked like one, in his heart he felt the change. With everything considered, he understood Franchize had given him the motivation for his new direction in life with his actions that day. Flaco owed him deeply and would do his best to repay that debt.

Franchize was grateful to have Evelyn gone. He grabbed the .38 special out of the stash in his crib. After last night he wasn't going to be riding around without a tool to get him out of a tight situation.

Things didn't make sense to him. Hitting the streets and putting his to ear the grapevine wasn't hard. Not drawing attention while doing so was. Stepping out the building this thoughts were interrupted. He noticed Flaco sleeping on the bench. People were walking by staring at him with disgust and it was a shame. Flaco happened to be family and to see him like that hurt. It's the ugly part of the game nobody wants to acknowledge. Anyone pushing the amount of work he used to could end up like this.

Walking into the parking lot, he got into his back up car and put the .38 in the stash. As he exited, Flaco popped in his rearview mirror waving his arms. Franchize didn't have time to deal with whatever issues Flaco might be having and decided to keep it moving. A car coming up his side of the street stopped him from turning. Looking back into his rearview mirror, he saw Flaco was almost at his car and changed his mind. He decided to lower his window and give the brother a minute out of respect.

"Flaco, what's up bro? I seen you sleeping on the bench over there. You got something on your mind?" By the time Franchize finished asking his questions, Flaco had caught his breath enough to let out, "Black Honda, stick up kid, plotting". Franchize let the words sink in. They clicked into place with so much force that all he could for the moment was "Get in". As Flaco closed the door, Franchize heightened his awareness in search for a black Honda. Checking the scene with more interest, he eased onto the street.

"Ayo Flaco, break down to me what know and how you know it." Flaco was excited for the first time in a long time for something other than a hit of crack. He talked to his old boss with the wisdom that can only be gained from years of living on the streets.

～　～　～

Misha was happy to see happy to see Evelyn. She wanted to get out of the hospital and back on track with her life. They went over the details concerning Creations and what needed to be done. The nurse came in with the discharge papers and said, "You're so lucky the trauma you sustained didn't cause a miscarriage".

"What? I think you got the wrong room. I'm Misha Davis."

"Yes, you are. I have your paperwork right here and you're pregnant."

Evelyn was so startled by the nurse's statement she blurted, "Bitch please, you know you buggin'! Did you check that twice?!" The nurse looked from Evelyn to Misha and said, "I beg your pardon if this if this news comes as a surprise. I thought you already knew. The fact of the matter is that are with child". With that being said, she scooped up the signed papers and left the room.

Evelyn, not knowing what else to say, grabbed a hold of Misha's good hand. She hoped with all her heart Misha never finds out what happened between her and Franchize. She knew Misha was Pro-life and believed in taking responsibility for her actions. Evelyn understood that no matter what happens between Misha and Franchize, her friend would get rid of the baby through abortion. She felt fake standing in support of her friend knowing what she did that morning and still tingling from it. The guilt was all the more real real when Misha checked her messages after they got outside. Out of nowhere she began to cry and broke down what was bothering her. Evelyn could only stare in amazement.

"The Detective that was looking into Franchize doesn't think he has been involved with anything wrong since he has been home. The guy who shot me is some crazy Federal Agent. Franchize is clean and I didn't trust him. I pushed him away. Now I have our baby in me and he hates me! Evelyn, I don't know what I'm going to do!"

With emotions still bouncing around inside of her, Evelyn saw this as chance to begin her redemption. Mustering up her courage she said, "Girl, don't kill yourself about not knowing. First chance you get, you let him know you're sorry and tell him there's a bun in the oven. That is when you're truly going to know where Franchize stands and if he is who you think he is".

CHAPTER 36

Franchize took Flaco to the office with him. After clearing his schedule for the next couple of

Days, Franchize jumped back on the road. In light of recent events, he started to look at the coincidences like pieces to the puzzle before him. Flaco's information gave him more questions than answers, but now he knew what to look for.

"Bro, it's real talk you been clean?" Franchize asked.

"Yea big bro. Reality kicked me in the head harder than a bull ever could" Flaco replied.

"You told me what you needed the money for. I got something even better. Do you want a job?"

"Not only do I want it, I need it big bro."

"Aight. Let's get you some work clothes and I got $500 for you to cover renting a room and getting to work until your paycheck drops."

They went to two stores on Steinway and had everything they needed. Going back to the whip, Franchize spotted two black Honda's.

"Ayo Flaco, you see the whip up the block and across the street?"

"Yea yea big bro. I seen them but the one across the street too new and the other one got a crashed bumper. The one I'm talking about is as old as that car but no crashed bumper." Wanting to have something more than a .38, he headed to a place where he knew he could get some fire power. Driving down 30th Avenue, he pulled in front of the Arab store people within the industry knew to sell baggies, scales and every type of drug accessory you could imagine.

"Big bro, want me to go in and get you something?" Flaco asked.

"Nah, I got it. Just look out for son." After Flaco confirmed he heard, Franchize walked into the store.

Yusef was a hard looking, short man with a long beard. He wore his pants legs hitched up so some ankle showed and always wore a kufi to match his sneakers. Upon seeing Franchize enter his store, Yusef's eyes lit up with recognition, but he held his excitement in check.

"My good brother Yusef, it's been a long time."

"Franchize my friend, you look healthy and that is a blessing."

"I need every type of blessing I can get right now. Can we talk?"

"Yes. Abdulla! Come run the register."

Finding out all Yusef had were grenades set back his plans to get extra power. Franchize didn't want to leave empty handed and snatched two of them at $500 a piece with two masks.

"Yo Franchize, we got a fish on the hook. Son following us. What's the move?" Flaco warned.

"Just be easy, I got this." Franchize drove down towards 21st Street. His crew had a construction project going and he knew some things that would play to his advantage. Pulling into the site, he told Flaco to stay put as he got out. Franchize made a show of greeting people and looking at equipment, and then slid off around to the back.

The alley behind the site ran the distance of the whole block. Seeing where the car was posted up gave an idea of many houses he had to pass to get behind the gunner. Creeping down the side of a two family brick house he put his mask on and pulled out the 38. These were movements from his past and it made him feel like he was back in the game. The consequences were real- life in prison if he got caught. His heart started racing. He saw the tail end of the car, Franchize tried to calm down. A couple walked past the entrance he was ready to spring out of. Even though they didn't look his way, their sudden appearance made his heart jump and beat even faster.

Moving live his life depended on it, he briskly walked, rounding the corner of the alley way. He pulled up beside the driver's door before he exhaled the deep breath he took. Franchize aimed the gun at the driver's head and said, "Hands on the steering wheel. You move them, you die." He had the drop he wanted. Using his left hand, he opened the driver's door.

"When I ask a question, you answer or you die."

"I no afraid of death puto."

He leveled the gun in his right hand the driver's head while he used his left to reach in and take the .357 revolver off of his lap.

"Why the fuck are you trying to kill me? If you want to play-dumb, two can play that." A quick strike brought a gun's butt down on the driver's head.

"We try again?

"If you gonna kill me, kill me. Running around flashing that watch like you don't know what's what? $100,000 on your head. Why you think I try to kill you puto? After I die another one come and fuck you."

Struck motionless with the maniac's words bouncing around in his head, Franchize thought about G Money. How G used to give the young girls crack and say his name was Franchize. He replayed the night G gave him the gun he used to catch the body that sent him up-state. Now he gave him a watch that had killers coming for his head. Franchize identified the source of his problems and it didn't matter why. He was ready to go.

"Listen papito. Today may be your lucky day. What's your name?"

"Cuco."

"You say the owner of this watch got 100,000 racks on my head. I don't have money. What I have is your life. Is it worth the paper?"

"No."

"Okay, if you tell me who put that money on my head and where I can find him, I will let you live." Cuco cocked his head to the side and looked up at Franchize thinking for a second.

"You don't know what person this watch belong to? You no steal this? Information no help you but whatever. Pay Day put money on your head. You let me live, Cuco owe you favor. Cuco owe nobody favor. You be lucky man. Nobody can buy Cuco favor. Call me and I give you details on where to find Pay Day and how to get him,"

Looking into Cuco's eyes he saw a ghost of light flicker across orbs so dark they could pass for black onyx spheres. "I believe you". How I reach you?" Smiling for the first time since they met, Cuco displayed a set of crooked, stained teeth.

"You don't have business card? Here take mine. You call; secretary pick up. Leave name and number and I get back to you. You no follow instructions, I no get back to you." Franchize took the card and Cuco closed the door. Pulling off his mask and putting the guns up, his gut told him he made a friend for life and found the snake living in his.

He dropped Flaco off and made his way to Creations. Franchize tossed around the idea of G Money setting him up. The more he did, the more sense it made. G had the same cruelty in him that motivated Big Boy behind the wall. His rules were his shield. The team was his everything. He went harder than he ever seen G in his life when it came to 2.24.

He didn't notice the gleam in Misha's eyes as she sat propped up with pillows. Franchize didn't care if she never wanted to see him again. He was going to still come in and continue his manicure routine. It would give him a couple of chances to fix things. But today his mind raced in a different direction. He broke down the GMB philosophy and the 2.24 foundation looking for what he could use to his advantage.

Knowing that my brother's hand will lay my life to rest if I violate this pledge, I take the responsibility of 2.24 into my mind body and spirit. Our cause is greater than one man. United we stand against all odds. A Dons word is law. We lay to rest all obstacles in the way of 2.24. Our religion is money and we find all ways to get it. If a Don is to fall at the hands of another mad, he who makes vengeance reality will become the next Don with his vision etched in fire on the hearts of all 2.24. One Don makes two Generals. Two Generals make four Bosses. Four Bosses makes eight Soldiers. Our numbers are our strength.

Franchize knew the pledge but the creed kept slipping through the cracks of his memory until he got it. *Violence is our sword and shield. Cash answers our prayers. Each man chosen is reflection of our soul. You are your brother's keeper. Our law is our law. From the head of 2.24 to the body of GMB, no man is above it. Our vision is a lifelong quest. To lose sight is to lose life.*

Everything started to fall into place for Franchize once he linked the pledge to the creed. A Don's word is law. He gave his word in the pledge and in the creed he helped create. It means he broke his own law in G Money's eyes. When he wrote that their vision was a lifelong quest, and that to lose sight is to lose life, he didn't mean it literally. United they stand against all odds. The cause is greater than one man. If one was to lose sight, he no longer took the responsibility of 2.24 into his mind, body and spirit. That meant his life was lost to the movement. That he longer took part of operations. G Money twisted it so that 2.24 become his keeper. With the politics involved, G probably gave him Pay Day's watch so that man could become his grim reaper. Both of Franchize's Generals died while he was in prison. G Money picked the next two Generals outside of protocol. He used the fact that he was in prison to claim adaptation due to unusual circumstances. This wasn't a two-way street. G Money could bend and break rules, but he couldn't fall back. Franchize understood what motivated G Money and he also knew the only option G left him.

Looking up he saw Misha was looking at him. There was something special about the moment and he couldn't grasp it. With so much on his mind, he didn't want to think about her harsh words. What confused him was the way her eyes held his every move. If she never wanted to see him again, she was doing a bad job of it. A glimmer of the memory of the first time he laid that pipe game down on Misha came to mind. It's been months since that night and he wondered if she could take dick right now all banged up like she was. As he toyed with the idea, he noticed her waving him over with her good arm. He thought about not going. His mind was all over the place and he needed to focus on a solution to other problems. Before he knew what he was doing, he stood in front of Misha appreciating how good she looked in her sweat pants and T-shirt. It looked like no matter what happened to her she would always be a cutie with a booty.

"Franchize, we need to talk. Can you take me home? I am letting Evelyn run the shop."

"Sure sweetheart. Let me help you up."

Making their way to the car Misha noticed how banged up Franchize was for the first time. She didn't want to comment on it. She felt it would start an argument and she needed to avoid that until she broke the news to him. What frightened her was feeling the gun on his waist for a brief second. He was going to be the father of their child and he chose now to start slipping up.

The gun made her mad but she felt safer at the same time. She asked herself if him strapping up was the result of the situation landing her in the hospital. Could this be his way of making sure she was protected and defended. Misha didn't want Franchize to go back to prison. So many questions swirled through her mind that she only realized they were at her apartment building when Franchize opened his door.

He didn't understand her mood swings. One minute she hated him and the next minute she was sweet. He knew it was fucked up, but he hoped the meds would keep her acting nice. Franchize sat down on the couch next to Misha and held her. Life had gotten so hectic the last couple of days that for the first time, it slowed down enough to show him he wasn't giving her the attention she deserved. Franchize kissed her forehead and silently hoped Evelyn would keep her mouth shut about their indiscretions. Misha finally spoke.

"Franchize, I Love you. I'm pregnant and I'm scared. I don't know what to do.

He pulled her closer and kissed her again not fully understanding her words. She shocked him with the unexpected combination of love and pregnancy. His brain slammed on the brakes. Thoughts of everything he wanted to do and say thrashed around his head then gently fell into place. He didn't want to be running around putting in work. Here sat a good woman telling him the best news he ever heard in his life and two obstacles threatened to take it all away from him. Those obstacles had to go. Nothing could jeopardize the life he envisioned during the years of his confinement. Only his actions would be his downfall. Franchize wanted to be the one responsible for his success or failure. Taking action could destroy his future but sitting back could end it. He knew the risks. He was ready to play with fire. Then a little thought grew. He could put his back to the hood and create a new positive vision with his family. It would be easy to pack up and go. Change his parole to another state.

His pride stood up before him and punched him in the mouth leaving a nasty taste behind at the thought of running away. The construction business grew every day. Misha's livelihood Creations had a hold of his girls heart. The paths his mind traveled led him back to the hood. Franchize accepted the road he chose. His enemies wanted war. He would give them a Gangsta's vision.

Looking at Misha's face in the light showed him how beautiful she was without makeup. Her features radiated love and sincerity even after being shot. He felt lucky to have such a strong positive woman by his side. He kissed her again.

"I love you more Misha. I love you now and the future you carry inside. We will make it happen as a family. This is the happiest day of my life. Trust me baby girl."

Misha smiled at Franchize's words and winced when he picked her up to lay her on the bed. He stayed with her for a while thinking and watching her sleep. G Money was no slouch and it seemed Pay Day had enough paper to make him consider killing his own self if he would have been able to collect the bounty after that. He knew it was time to get to work. He left Misha sleeping. He looked back for a brief second taking in her pure beauty. Franchize realized the happiest day of his life also happened to be his saddest. All in one day he found out he would be a father and that his best friend, one he considered a brother, had lined him up to get killed.

If this wasn't a roller coaster ride, Franchize really didn't know what was.

Parked up with the stash spot open, he used his ear piece to try and call G Money while he cleaned the bullets for the .38 and .357 with baby wipes.

The thin leather gloves he had on made his hands feel a little clumsy as he took care of the bullets and guns.

"What's shaking bro?" G Money asked as he picked up.

"I need to see you," Franchize said plainly.

"You good? You sound funny."

"Shit got live. I'm tight and naked."

"You really was going straight when you gave me your clothes?"

"Yea. Now I'm kicking myself in the ass for that. I need help."

"You're my brother and I got you. Whatever you need! You want me to bring you an outfit to wear?"

"Yea. I need that ASAP. Can you meet me by Con Ed in a half?"

"Give me 45 and I got you, ya dig?" Franchize grunted a reply and hung up

G Money grinned as the thoughts of his newly developed plan came into focus. The bitch ass nigga Franchize didn't even have a hammer with him. Pay Day put that unexpected $100,000 on his head and some extra change never hurt nobody. G Money got ready to make his move and mentally explored the different ways he could push Franchize's back. His brother just got caught and he could understand why he wanted to meet at Con. Ed. It was on the Queens side of the East River. Quiet, get low type of spot and now that it was nighttime, the place would be deserted. He laughed out loud as it hit him, Franchize dug his own grave and here he sat loading the same .45 Franchize gave him to finish the job. Checkmate mothafucka.

G Money drove into the parking lot across the street from Con Ed. It was attached to apartment buildings and had easy access to the side street. He saw where Franchize's car was and liked the spot. He happened to be between a SUV and a Minivan on the only wall in the lot. He parked up close by and got the .45 out. There was no point in making a family reunion out of this and airing out dirty laundry. He made his way over with gun close to his body. His black jeans and hoodie let him blend into the asphalt glided over. Making his way to the passenger side of Franchize's car, the quiet neighborhood, exploded with the sound of "Bang! Bang! Bang!" in rapid succession. After a brief pause, another "Bang!".

Franchize let those shots loose as soon as he stepped out from behind the SUV. He stood over G Money and put another bullet in his head. Every time he squeezed the trigger from the .357, it was like thunder strikes. Every blast did so much damage that after the first three shots he was already dead. The fourth one was to make sure the brother who betrayed him had a closed casket.

Going through G Money's pockets produced his phone. Looking around for G Money's car keys made him start to panic because he couldn't find them. He noticed the .45 on the floor and picked it up. Running to G Money's black Impala, he found it on with the keys in the ignition. He hit the code on G Money's special alarm box and this time he knew he had less than a minute. Speeding out and turning down towards the East River, a cop car with its siren blaring flew out from a side street and turned right behind him.

Franchize's heart started to race. He became aware of the three guns he has on him. All of a sudden they started to weigh heavy. The .357 had a fresh body it and the .38 with the .45 were the icing on the cake that would give him enough years in prison to make a Miami Heat final score look like nothing. He pulled over and checked the .45 to make sure there was one in the head. Franchize kept repeating to himself that he wasn't going back to prison. He made his decision to hold court right here in the streets.

As soon as the officers stepped out of their car, the blast from an explosion crashed into their ear drums like a tsunami. They turned in the direction of terrorist attack and saw fires race up the side of a brick building from a parking lot a black and a half away. Without even thinking about it, both officers jumped back in their car and made a u-turn to face in the direction of all the commotion.

Breathe! Nigga, you better start breathing and driving at the same damn time. Fuck are you waiting for? The words roared within Franchize's mind. As he made his way to get rid of the .357, he fully comprehended how disastrous things could have gotten a second ago. Franchize looked up as he got out the car in front of his building He asked himself what happened to the square life he wanted to live. He knew the average bozo would of called police to handle their problems. Lames used to call 911 for back up, but he couldn't see himself doing that ever, no matter how much he wanted to change. Trying to live a square life was turning out to be harder than he ever thought possible. He knew he had to work it. It's what he had his mind set on. It's what he was going to be right after he took care of his problems.

Looking at the streets around him, Franchize recognized this was where he practiced the morally negative concepts that destroyed his life long ago. This was where he bankrupted his soul so that progression to a prison cell became his next chapter in life. And here he sat risking the freedom he craved all those years. He knew what needed to be done and what he wants to do were two different beasts. At this level in the game, Franchize could only keep his own council but he couldn't make the next steps become reality by himself. It was common to confide your thoughts to someone close to you then end up doing 25 to life. Loyalty couldn't be bought, but must be earned. Things needed to be done! Any way he put it, shit was fucked up so now it became his responsibility to act and protect his own life, Misha's, and the future she held within her womb. At peace with his decision, Franchize formulated a plan.

CHAPTER 37

"**Y**ou need to call him and tell him now!" Negro's wife Rosa demanded. Full of energy, she paced back and forth using her annoying high pitched voice to strike at Negro's nerves.

"I am going to tell him. He has a lot his on plate. That's why he hasn't been able to help out lately." Negro just looked at her heels click over and over on the hardwood floors.

"You're going to do this in front of me. I am your wife, the mother of our kids. We are your family. You need to get it through that thick skull that your brother and sister are your siblings. They are your relatives with me and our kids as your family and first priority. Working twelve hour days seven days a week won't fly with me. Especially when he doesn't do shit and gets the same money! Are you crazy? Demand a bigger share of the profits and that he work too. This is our business and your family needs you."

Negro looked at Rosa and knew he would never hear the end of her arguments for more money. Ever since Quality Construction Co. became a big hit expanding and always locking in big contracts, she kept looking for a way to cut Franchize out. Rosa even held the original ownership documents to argue Franchize wasn't a partner until he showed her the new paperwork. Negro knew she was to look out for their best interests in her own twisted way. If he wanted to have peace at home, he had to do something.

"Baby, go get my phone."

Franchize stood in his brother's home office and noticed how the papers were stacking up. "Franchize, we need to work out some of the responsibilities. I'm going crazy with all the administrative work and book keeping. I'm constantly needed to supervise from site to site so everything goes right and making sure we don't have employee's sitting around. I need you to do your share."

"How about I take over administrative and secretarial work? Let's hire a bookkeeper to get everything in order for our accountant. I will get all the bills out and run down the late payers and make sure all our insurances and licenses are up to date. Simply let me take over everything technical with computers and dealing with the paperwork. Give me a week to restructure everything then I can help out with site checks. We got a deal?"

Negro couldn't believe his luck. Most of his time was tied up with administrative work. Now he could go back to eight hour work days six days a week and spend Sundays at home. If this didn't make Rosa happy, he didn't know what to tell her. *She was right about having a talk with Franchize.*

"You got a deal bro. Whatever you need to take from here to do what has to be done, just grab it. Ima let Rosa know cause I gots to run."

Standing in the middle of Negro's office made him think about the huge task before him. Pulling out his phone he called Billy's daughter Angela who ran the company's website.

"Hey Angela, I need your help. How could we source out all of our administrative work without crazy costs? Does your magic net have that answer?" Franchize heard Angela laughing.

"Actually it does. It's called virtual assistants and independent consultants. Anything you want could be done could be for a cost. It's actually cheaper to go this way."

"Okay. We need a bookkeeper to have things organized for our accountant. I want you to get the people needed to run an effective office and check our licenses, insurances, and virtual security. Take the money from share of the profits at first then transition them into the company's operation expenses account.

I got a two grand bonus I'm leaving in cash in an envelope on my brother's desk. You just earned a raise from $1,500 every two weeks to $1,000 a week and you're in charge of this project. We clear?"

"Yes sir. I'm going to need access to your office on Northern Boulevard and I need all the paperwork with access to the computer."

"Okay, I'm going to text you my brother's address with instructions for his wife to let you do what has to be done in here. If you need help, hire an assistant. You have full authority to get this project done. I'm counting on you. Check in with me in a week for a progress report."

"Boss, you won't be disappointed. I promise."

Franchize knew Angela was better than him at handling tasks like this. He couldn't tackle everything himself. His thoughts started to race and he looked up only to see Rosa staring at him.

"You think you're slick. You tricked your brother."

Franchize looked puzzled and then she continued. "You said you're taking over all this work, but you're just having someone else do it. You lied. You do nothing while he kills himself working." Rosa acted like she had a huge fierce spirit trapped in a petite girly frame. Franchize couldn't do anything but smile.

"Rosa, how do think this instant success happened?" Before she could respond he continued. "Responsibility and decision making comes with leadership. The girl I just put in charge of these tasks looks like a gothic misfit."

Rosa rolled her eyes but before she could say anything, Franchize kept talking. "She is also the one who made this success possible. A multi-million dollar company is what we are going to be before the year is out. All thanks to her. She is soon to be a minority owner of this company. Talent like that comes by you once in a lifetime. Leadership skills allow me to see if she is equipped to handle this workload Therefore, my decision to delegate these tasks is sound. It's all about maintaining a high standard and making money. This way your kids, alongside my own on the way, can live a comfortable life. I love brother and we are all going to do what we are best at so that the money continues to roll in. Now you heard me invite Angela over here." Franchize pulled out his office keys and stack of crispy hundred dollar bills. Counting off the $2,000 promised, he picked up an envelope off Negro's desk and put the keys and money in it. He took a marker and wrote Angela's name on it. Dropping it on the table, he strolled by the stunned Rosa and let himself out.

~ ~ ~

"Uncle Tito, I need another car. I want the black Maxima over there."

"Nephew, I don't know if you think I'm crazy or something like that, but I watch the news too. Maybe I think your money's bad for business."

"Just name your price Uncle Tito."

~ ~ ~

After his meeting with Cuco, Franchize parked in front of Misha's building. He sat there with his thoughts in a million different places. The Pay Day situation bothered him and he knew the man must go, but if anything went wrong he could be the one going to the grave or prison. Misha being pregnant complicated things for him. Franchize always told himself that if a woman was having his child he would be there for the baby's birth, first step, and first word. To be a father and do everything he didn't get growing up.

If he let Pay Day run around with $100,000 on his head he would be putting his family at risk and might not live through the next attack himself. If he got caught, he would be stepping on principles and hurting the child more than anything. It could be death of him and his family if he did nothing or the fate of living tortured if he got arrested. There was no half-assing this type of lifestyle. After this was over, he would use his pivot foot to change directions. It no longer made sense to travel into the realm of death and prison,

CHAPTER 38

Lying in bed with Misha, Franchize felt something more than love. Her very being had a magical effect on him. With her body so close, he could feel she was more than soft and warm. Misha became his everything. Franchize didn't want to admit it to himself, but he knew he would end up marrying her.

He wanted to make sure the groundwork for their evolution was laid. He turned to Misha and asked, "Where are we going from here?". Misha held Franchize's gaze and asked herself if she loved him.

"I don't know where we go from here Franchize and that scares me. My heart is running towards you and my mind is telling me it's chasing a thunder cloud. I guess my head and heart never truly understood that lightning could strike cause it did. Not only do I love you, I'm keeping our baby."

"Misha, I knew I was sick when my soul sat on a frozen riverbank. You are the spring it waited for. I no longer feel cold inside. Every time I look at you, the warmth you brought into my life shows itself. I existed in a lost land until you sparked a vision that drew me to you. You inspire me to want to be the best father ever. I will give you my everything. Just promise to always stand by side."

Misha couldn't believe what she was hearing. The way Franchize spoke made her feel genuine love in every word. Did she truly find a man she could love for the rest of her life?

"I promise to always stand by your side. I fell in love with you the first time you saved me on those stairs and I didn't even know it. I want you to move in with me."

Franchize didn't know how to respond to Misha's request so he kissed her. All she had on was a long T-shirt and he couldn't keep his hands from exploring her soft curves. He remembered he had to be careful with her injuries. His desire drove him forward. His fingers found her wet entrance. Deepening the kiss, his tongue danced with hers. As he continued with his hand, he felt her juices running down the side of his palm. The juicy juice exploration excited him and his mouth found her neck. His extension bulged and demanded attention. He kissed and touched her until he couldn't take it anymore. Climbing on top of her, he sunk his shaft into her. As he delivered long slow strokes she dug her nails into his shoulder inciting a tantalizing sensation. She was so wet and warm inside that Franchize got lost finding his way in and out of her. The glory of her body held him captive. Looking into her eyes, Franchize sensed the love and lust in them. They spoke of a loyalty and devotion he could trust. Breathing in her essence, he exhaled the words, "I Love you". The friction her sweet spot created with his strokes melted his resistance. All the backed up frustration shot out of him while deep inside of his baby girl. Staying buried in her another moment allowed him to realize the missing piece that was necessary to fill the void in his life was laying right beneath him.

When Franchize left Misha's apartment, she was fast asleep. With the mission on his mind, he couldn't continue to hold her in his arms. He hoped she liked the poem he wrote for her on the pad next to her computer. One last time he told himself, after this he would go condo shopping with Misha. No point in renting when they both made enough money to buy a place. Too much dirt had been done on these streets for him to continue living them.

Getting close to Pay Day's location forced him to slip into a focused state of mind that could have rivaled a monk's. It was time to put in that work.

You're either on point or being made out to be a point. Pulling over, he got out and jumped into Cuco's black car. "This is what I promised to get you for the job," Franchize said passing Cuco a grenade.

"That some gangsta shit. I take care of that thing no problem." Cuco grinned is as he rubbed the grenade. "Just be where I told you to be."

"You sure he's gonna be at that spot?" Franchize wanted to make sure Cuco`s info was sharper than a scalpel.

"I watch the money. Pay Day sweet. He never change. He think he safe out here. I get hungry so I want money to put in my safe. Lots of money. I don't kill for free. Always for a fee. I owe you but we even after this."

Franchize left Cuco in position and got back behind the steering wheel of his Maxima. Pay Day walked out of his stash house off of Jackson Avenue in the Bronx with over $300,000 in a book bag. He didn't trust anybody meeting the connect. Breaking down bricks of heroine left more money behind than he knew what to do with it. Another year or two of flipping like this and he would retire to a mansion down south. All the things he wanted to do in life preoccupied his mind until a blast up the block stunned him. Looking for the source of the noise, he spotted the 7 Series BMW that held his back up crew smoking. All of its windows were blown out and he knew he had to get out of there. Nervous and fearing for his life, Pay Day fumbled with the door handle of the truck when a black car skidded to a halt trapping in the double parked Range. A man in a black hoodie and mask shot his driver in the head through the open window.

Pay Day turned around and started running trying to make his way back into the house. A mean slug to his back spun him around and he fell on the steps. His bag went flying. His brother D Day scrambled out the passenger side when the Range blew up. His baby brother lay stretched out on the floor with the .9 mm still in his hand. The hooded figure jumped on the hood of the car behind the Range and came down through the smoke onto the sidewalk. He saw D Day starting to get up. The hooded figure moved fast towards him. Pay Day tried to scramble backwards up the steps, but every movement hurt so much that he thought he was going to black out any second. Then his eyes focused on the barrel of a cannon and watched it explode into his face.

~ ~ ~

Cuco looked at the next victims in this life smoke. He pulled the pin to the grenade and let go of the trigger. Instead of throwing it right away, he held it. The risk he was taking excited him. After a brief pause, he tossed it hard and it hit homeboy sitting in the back seat right in the mouth while he took a pull. Moving on, he got into place to handle the next part of his mission.

Hearing the explosion put Franchize into motion cutting off the Range. He hopped out and shot the driver in the head with the .45 then ducked down pulling the pin on the grenade he tossed into the Range. He saw Pay Day was making a run for it and clapped him in the back with the monster he held. Getting low behind his car, the explosion passed making his ears ring. Dazed for a second before the waves of clarity hit him at full force, the thought of a prison sentence pushed him harder. Energy flowed into Franchize and through the smoke he jumped on the hood of the car between him and his target.

Running down on Pay Day, he put two in his face. Spinning to run off, he saw a gun pointed at him. Diving before the gunman could get a shot off, he landed in a bunch of garbage bags by the basement of the house. The sound of shots ringing out made him feel confined to this narrow area. Spotting a book bag, he moved a garbage bag to get it and found a woman holding on to it. That's when he saw his mask on the floor. His emotions started raging when he noticed she was pregnant. He asked himself why the mask had to come off. She looked scared to death. She was pregnant. Would she testify against him in court? He told himself he couldn't do it before his survival instincts took over. Boom. Boom. Twice to the chest leaving her crumpled in front of the basement door. He told himself over and over as he put the mask back on that he would leave behind no witnesses no matter what. She was a casualty of war.

Creeping up the steps, he looked back and no longer wanted the money. He left it in her arms. Checking to see where the last shooter was at, he spotted him limping down the block. Getting back on the sidewalk, he emptied the clip into the man's back. Tossing the .45 into his car, he hit the timer on his remote and took off running down the street towards Cuco who was backing down the one way.

"Where is the bag?" were the first words out of Cuco's mouth when he jumped into the car. "I don't know. Shit get fucked up back there. More people died than had to and..."

Boom! Franchize looked back before they turned the corner and another man was lying in the middle of the street.

~ ~ ~

"Tina, why must you be so nosey every time you hear something happening outside?"

"Carlos, I'm just making sure those crazies out there don't mess up the garbage. Last week they gave us a summons because you didn't let me check. Don't worry. Stop being so overprotective," Tina said as she walked out.

Carlos was tired of his wife's crazy obsession to be in everyone's business. He got up and put his pants on. Looking for his other sneaker, he heard another explosion and then gun shots. After making sure the kids were in their rooms, he walked right into the worst scene he could have ever imagined. His wife's body lay at the bottom of the steps. Blood poured from her like a river spilling on to dry land. Carlos screamed in agony at the sight of his pregnant wife. Her hand clutched a book bag and he knew she was already dead. He knelt down next to her and thought she died for nothing- all because some punks didn't know how to shoot. Why didn't she listen to him? In anger, he grabbed the book bag out of her hand and slammed it against the wall then threw it on the ground. A stack of money tied with rubber bands tumbled into the blood before him. Stunned for a second, he wondered about the future of his 3 kids. He went to the bag and looked in where the zipper had started to open. He saw more money in one place than ever before in his life. He looked at the wad on the floor soaking up his wife's blood and decided not to touch that stack of already bloody money. The bag he held was another story. Carlos took it and stashed it in the apartment. After calling the police, he went back to hold his wife. The shame, anger and deep loss he felt within was too much for Carlos to handle as he began to cry.

Cuco crossed the Triborough Bridge and pulled over. "I go no more. Get out," Cuco said still fuming at the fact that Franchize did not recover the money. He didn't want to talk or hear anything else on the subject.

Franchize noticed the no nonsense tone and got out to walk towards his crib. He still had a couple of blocks to go flooded when a burning desire to take a piss flooded his system. Franchize looked around and saw that the coast was clear. It was four in the morning and he figured nobody would be paying any attention to him relieving himself. Emptying his bladder felt so that he closed his eyes for a second. When he opened them, the flashing lights of a blue and white cop car scorched his eyes. The spot light was on him illuminating what he doing.

Thinking quickly he knew he was clean and that this was only a ticket. The only problem was that he didn't have any I.D. on him and they could run him through the system. Police contact meant a parole violation, Fixing himself, he looked over his shoulder at the two uniformed cops. They looked like Pinky and the Brain. "*Fuck it*," was his last thought as he booked it.

Sprinting down the block with everything he had pumping into his legs he went flying. Franchize knew he fast and the little lead he had should only extend. That's why he was shocked when he was tripped from behind.

Officer Alonzo Grant was slim and lean because he ran three miles every other day and usually sprinted the last block of his run. He was a natural born runner and enjoyed the freedom it gave him. When the perp took off that surge adrenaline he loved found itself racing through his blood. Picking up ground with every step, he closed the distance before the block ended. The perp was deceptively quick, but all he had to do was tap the back of his heel. He watched the man trip up causing him to go flying through the air.

Franchize landed with the full force of the impact on his chest. A spasm of pain shot through his core. His lungs fought for air. Panic started to set in and being hurt became the least of his worries. He tried to get up, but his oxygen depleted and his body buckled. The skinny cop, that Pinky in the face ass nigga, was on his back putting the cuffs on and he hated the feeling of being of being busted over some lame lemon shit.

Franchize made it through the system in record time. It looked like a slow day on busts and he got lucky. Sliding through the cracks, he plead guilty and took the community service. When he left the courthouse, he decided not to tell his parole officer. There would be no point in snitching on himself. Police contact at 4 am was a sure violation. The only thing left to do would be to see if his overworked parole officer noticed his blip on her radar.

After coming out the shower, Franchize laid his sore body to down to rest. He thought about all the people he killed since coming home. The cycle of violence crept up and continued to besmirch his second chance. During the years he spent inside prison, Franchize could have sworn on a bible that he had things figured out. The abuse and destruction of the community he lived in just ended up taking a new form. He willed his mind to adapt to the new set of circumstances set before him and find a way to break the chain that weighed him down in these rough waters.

What hurt Franchize the most is the image of the pregnant woman. It was burned into his psyche. Not only did he kill her, but he probably killed her unborn child all in the name of self preservation. He asked himself what he had become. His mind answered with the echo of, "Monster, *"A relentless murderer thinking only about himself"*.

The images of his sister and Misha appeared before him. He wondered what he would do if someone harmed the two pregnant women in his life. He knew right then and there that he wouldn't be able to shrug that off. They could never be thought of as casualties of war. Silently, he prayed. He begged forgiveness for all he had done. What he prayed for the most was for his sister and Misha's safety. He did not want them to be hurt in any kind of way because of him. He hoped Misha wouldn't overreact to the news of his possible violation. With so much going on in his life, Franchize just wanted to be done with all the negativity and focus on the good. He mentally organized his to-do list, finding himself in a dream laced with fears and joys, with pain and pleasure, with hate and love taking him on a roller coaster ride he could have never imagined existed.

A knock on the door woke him. At first he was mad at the interruption of the experience he was having, but upon seeing who was at the door, his anger quickly disappeared. Misha stood there in a sweat suit that highlighted her curves. "Franchize, I've been trying to reach you. Are you okay? You look banged up. What happened?"

"Sweetheart, I have to tell you something. Sit down baby. Yesterday, I got arrested for pissing in the street and not having any I.D. on me. It was after curfew and I could get violated by parole. I just don't know yet." Franchize stared into Misha's innocent face and a wave of love swelled within him. She didn't look mad or disappointed in him. She looked like he hoped she would- calm, caring and concerned for him.

Misha was relieved to hear it was this and not him leaving her. She got up on her tippy toes and kissed Franchize. "Whatever it is, we can work it out." His heart vibrated with the affection her words radiated. His hands squeezed the round section of her back while he kissed her deeply. Turning her around, he rubbed himself backside so she could feel what stood at full attention. Kissing her neck and letting his hands find their way under her sweater turned him on even more. A hunger to devour her growled from within him.

Misha started to grind her backside against Franchize and it drove him crazy. Using his thumbs, he pushed her sweatpants and thong down in one swift motion. Misha in time with Franchize had the source of his power in her hand and over his boxers. She took him and guided his strength to her hot, dripping gateway to pleasure. Franchize was stuck by her actions. The need to be deep inside her fiercely urged him forward. Before he could finish his first stroke, Misha threw it back, devouring the shaft of his manhood. They connected with blinding intensity.

The tight wetness pulled on him. Called him. Enticed and danced within him. Franchize pounded her pussy harder as her moans got louder. Misha used her good arm to hold on to the side of the couch. It afforded her the leverage she wanted to throw her pussy onto Franchize creating a beat all of their own. Before he could get himself under control, he let loose deep inside his wonder woman.

Misha turned around and got on knees so she could clean Franchize off with her mouth. All Franchize could think about were those lips... the strokes of her tongue… the gentle sucking that kept him at full force. Wanting to return the favor before round two began, he led Misha to the bedroom.

CHAPTER 39

"Sit down Mr. Montenegro," said his parole officer Ms. Johnson with a weird look in her eyes. "How's everything going? Anything to report?"

Franchize thought about her statement and it was the first time in a long time she came at him like this. He felt she was giving him a hint to come clean about the arrest. The criminal inside of him whispered in his head that only a fool tells on himself. The more he tossed that concept around in his head, the more sense it made. The code of silence was a part of his own and he wasn't able to give it up.

"No, Ms. Johnson. Everything is fine."

Franchize heard her sigh with disappointment. "Give me a second Mr. Montenegro."

When Ms. Johnson left the room, he knew something was wrong. Grabbing the phone off her table, he called Misha and let her know the situation. After hanging up, the urge to run entered him. He brushed that aside and resolved to overcome whatever was his new obstacle.

When Ms. Johnson came back with cops handcuffs in hand, he knew his fate.

"I wish you would have told me about the police contact Mr. Montenegro. I would have worked with you. I believe you still need to learn a thing or two about taking responsibility for your actions. Do you have anything to say?" she asked.

"No."

~ ~ ~

Franchize waited on the bus to go up north. Since he was a Category One felon, his minimum on a violation was one year. With 5 years of post release supervision hanging over his head, he knew that if he fought the violation, they would give up to two years or better. Thankfully, luck ended up on his side after all. They offered him a program called Willard that was only 97 days long. If he failed to complete it, he would have to do the year. In his eyes, it was a no brainer. 97 days of bullshit or a year of bullshit. Misha wasn't going anywhere and he would still make it home in time for the baby's birth. Things were looking good.

Angela took over his responsibilities at the company. He was able to talk his brother into giving up five percent of his share in the company to add to the ten percent of his he was using to supply Angela's salary. She became a 1.5% percent owner and she earned it. She put in crazy work and kept the company expanding at such a rate it became hard to imagine where things would be when he came home. The success was an accident. He didn't completely understand how it happened, but at this stage in the game it didn't matter. His family was safe and he would be home soon.

"Montenegro! Visit!" the C.O. barked. He knew it wasn't Misha because she only came on Fridays and the weekends while he was waiting to go up top. Curious to see who it was, he got dressed.

"Stacey? What the fuck you doing here? I don't got time for your shit! Deuces," Franchize said as he prepared to walk off. Stacey started crying and drew attention from other tables in the 4 Building visiting room.

"Franchize. I'm so sorry. Please forgive me. It was Fats. He tricked me. He raped me and made me tell him."

"Fuck is you talking 'bout? What does Fats got to do with this visit? Make some damn sense or get the fuck out of here."

"Fats made me tell him where your sister lives since he couldn't get to you. I think he killed her. I don't know what to do."

"Shut the fuck up. That's what you're going to do. If my sister is dead, that fat fuck raping your dirty ass doesn't make this shit right."

With the tears still streaming down her cheeks, Franchize got up, grabbed her hair and spit in her face. He shoved her away like she had Ebola. He had to get on the phone.

"C.O., this visit is over. I gots to get back to the block," Franchize said.

"Okay tough guy. You like to treat women like that, then tell me the fucking obvious and think I'm going to jump to your tune? Have a seat and you will get back to the block when I feel like letting you go back. One more word to me and you're going to be in the why-me cell all night still waiting tough guy."

Hearing confirmation from his brother's crying voice made Franchize's heart turn into a block of ice. He silently vowed to exact revenge as rage consumed him. Looking around and seeing bars holding him in created an overflow of hatred and anger. Not being able to do anything at this point in time destroyed a part of Franchize he didn't think he could get back.

The thirst for Fats' blood kept his eyes dry while the wrathful volcano that had replaced his cold heart pumped hot, seething lava through his veins. His mind thought of all of the things he wanted to do to

Fats and he let the thoughts consume him. Pausing in his pacing, he realized it was a plan that formulated itself. He knew what he was going to do. Franchize was going back to the hood and he'd show Fats how a real gangsta takes his revenge.

To be continued...

Coming Soon

Back to the Hood: A Gangsta's Revenge

Letter from an editor to her author-

Mi amor-

Thank you so much for this opportunity. It has truly been a pleasure polishing the story you brought to life. I look forward to seeing this book make its first rounds bring its readers the same gasps, emotions, rage, and tenderness of heart that it brought to me with every page. I see so much potential in this trilogy and hope that you'll continue to let me ride shotgun on this wild ride. While Franchize is currently on my shit list, I came to love the well-intentioned fool and solo queria lo major para el. I know you want to churn out two more books so he may have a little bit more to learn before he goes back to being the ideal citizen, but I can't wait to see where you take him. It's been real!

Sincerely,
Amy Cecilia 😉

Made in the USA
Middletown, DE
05 February 2023

.00126